More Tales to Give You

Goosebumps

Ten Spooky Stories
Special Edition 2

R.L. Stine

Contents

Hippo

Scholastic Children's Books,
Commonwealth House, 1–19 New Oxford Street, London WC1A 1NU, UK
a division of Scholastic Ltd
London ~ New York ~ Toronto ~ Sydney ~ Auckland

First published in the USA by Scholastic Inc., 1995
First published in the UK by Scholastic Ltd, 1997
Copyright © Parachute Press Inc., 1996

GOOSEBUMPS is a trademark of Parachute Press, Inc.

ISBN 0 590 19567 0

Typeset by Rowland Phototypesetting Ltd, Bury St Edmunds, Suffolk
Printed by Cox & Wyman Ltd, Reading, Berks.

10 9 8 7 6 5 4 3 2 1

THE WEREWOLF'S
FIRST NIGHT

"What's the problem, Brian?" my dad asked, peering at me in the rearview mirror. "We've been on the road for four hours, and you haven't said two words. Aren't you excited?"

"Sure, Dad." I scrunched down in the seat of the car. That way, he couldn't see my face. He couldn't see that I was lying.

We were driving to Thunder Lake. We go to Thunder Lake every summer. It's a holiday resort, with cabins, a golf course, a big lake, and some other stuff.

Lots of families go there because they have a camp for the kids. The grown-ups dump their kids in the camp. Then they play golf or hang out in the clubhouse.

"Are you sure you're okay, Brian?" Dad asked.

"Leave him alone, honey," my mum said. "Brian's probably a tiny bit nervous about being in the teen camp this summer."

Nervous wasn't the right word. *Terrified* was more like it.

Dad cleared his throat. He always clears his

throat before he gives me a pep talk. "Look at it this way, Brian. The teen camp will help you get over your shyness. You'll feel more grown-up being with older kids. Anyway, you belong there. You're twelve years old now . . ."

That's right, I thought. I'm twelve years old. And I'd like to live to see *thirteen*!

"You're going to have a great time," Dad insisted.

"I know you're scared now," Mum told me. "But the time is coming when you won't be afraid of anything. Just wait and see."

Mum and Dad had it all wrong. Sure, the teen camp made me a little nervous.

But what made me afraid were the stories about Thunder Lake. Stories about creatures in the night. About howls and shrieks, and enormous footprints.

About werewolves living by the lake.

I've been hearing those stories since we started spending our holidays at Thunder Lake six years ago. I've been really scared ever since. And that really annoys my parents.

My parents think I'm a wimp.

So I keep my mouth shut about the stories.

But I'm still scared.

"There's the ten-mile sign!" Dad called out.

I sat up straight and stared out of the window. Sure enough, the sign said THUNDER LAKE: TEN MILES.

Next came the five-mile sign.

Time was running out.

Finally I spotted the sign I'd been dreading: WELCOME TO THUNDER LAKE! A FAMILY RESORT. SWIMMING. HIKING. BOATING. GOLF. TENNIS.

And werewolves.

The teen camp had ten kids in it. A guy named Kevin was the only other twelve-year-old. He and I were the youngest.

Kevin had red hair and the whitest skin I've ever seen. The older guys made fun of him because his mother forced him to smear on lots of lotion to keep from getting sunburned.

I have brown hair and eyes, and my skin doesn't burn. So they don't joke about the way I look. But I'm short and a bit clumsy. And that's what they make fun of.

The three oldest guys were the toughest. Jake, Phil and Don. They were all fifteen.

Jake had dark curly hair and a gold earring in one ear. Phil had beady blue eyes and always wore a red Bulls T-shirt. Don was short, wide and mean.

"If I had the guts, I'd call him Fatso," Kevin whispered to me one day during a baseball game.

"Yeah," I whispered back. "But he'd sit on you and squash you to death."

When it was my turn to bat, I trotted to the plate. Don was the catcher. When he saw me he called, "Easy out!"

Then he grinned.

And I froze.

I'd never seen Don smile before. So I'd never seen his teeth.

But I could see them now.

They were the longest front teeth I'd ever seen in my life. And they were sharp.

Like fangs.

Like a wolf's fangs.

Then Don did something strange. He shut his mouth real quick and turned his head away.

As if he'd forgotten he wasn't supposed to smile.

I swallowed and licked my lips. Every second I stood at the plate, I expected to feel his fangs stick into my leg.

When I struck out, Don grinned again. I couldn't believe it! His teeth looked normal. His fangs were gone!

But I knew I hadn't imagined them.

Then I remembered the stories about werewolves. They started out as humans. They didn't change into wolves all at once. But on the night of the full moon — total werewolf!

Could Don be a werewolf?

After the game, I told Kevin about Don's teeth. Then I waited for him to laugh. But he didn't.

"Man!" he said. "I heard all the stuff about this lake and families changing into werewolves. But I didn't really believe it. Are you sure it wasn't a trick?"

"I guess it could have been," I admitted. "But

if he wanted to scare me, why did he try to hide the fangs?"

"Yeah," Kevin agreed. "We'd better be careful when the full moon comes."

Later, I looked up the dates of the moon on Mum's little pocket calendar.

Only four nights until the next full moon!

I wanted to tell Mum and Dad how afraid I was. Afraid Don would come after me. But I didn't want them to get on my case about being such a wimp.

So I didn't say anything. Not even when they went to play cards at the clubhouse and left me alone in the cabin.

I kept telling myself that there were no such things as werewolves. That Don was just a kid.

Everything was quiet for a while. Then I heard rustling outside the cabin.

My heart started pounding. But I told myself it was a squirrel.

The rustling grew louder.

My knees began to shake. I told myself it was a raccoon.

I heard a low growl right outside the door. Then scratching sounds, and another growl.

I told myself it was Don.

I shut off the lights and peered out of the front window. The moon lit up the darkness. In the distance, I saw something red moving through the trees towards the lake.

A red Bulls T-shirt.

Phil! Running through the woods like a wild animal!

As soon as Mum and Dad came back, I told them. I didn't care how wimpy I sounded.

"Oh, Brian, don't you get it?" Dad asked. "The guys are just playing a trick on you. They know you're scared, and they're taking advantage of it!"

"I know it's hard not to be scared, dear," Mum said. "But it will all change soon. Trust me."

"Your mother's right," Dad agreed. "I'm surprised you fell for that trick, Brian. Don't you realize how easy it is for someone to sneak up to a cabin and make a few scary sounds?"

Okay, so it's easy to make scary sounds and growls.

But how easy is it to make wolf tracks?

Because that's what I found the next morning.

Not regular wolf tracks.

These paw prints were at least ten inches long!

I found them in the dirt around the cabin and followed them until they disappeared into the woods — at the exact spot where I'd seen Phil the night before.

Phil was a werewolf, too. No doubt about it.

A couple of nights later, the teen camp had a cookout by the lake. I didn't want to go. But since the moon wasn't full yet, I figured I'd be okay.

After we ate hamburgers and toasted marshmallows, we all sat around the campfire. Jake told a spooky story about some guy with a hook for a hand.

I didn't pay much attention. A guy with a hook for a hand didn't scare me. Werewolves did.

I kept my eyes on Don and Phil. The firelight threw weird shadows on their faces. It turned their eyes blood-red. I expected them to start growing fangs and claws any minute.

But nothing happened.

When the cookout was over, we started along the path towards the cabins. Suddenly, I realized I'd forgotten my new jacket. Mum would kill me if I left it out in the sand all night. So I ran back to get it.

The moon lit up the dark beach. I saw a figure kneeling in the sand. When he lifted his head to the sky, something glinted in the moonlight.

Jake's gold earring.

As I watched, Jake held his arms up towards the moon, opened his mouth, and howled.

The bloodcurdling howl of a wolf.

I knew no human could howl like that! I turned and ran up the path as fast as I could.

I caught up with Kevin. "Kevin, did you hear that howl?" I gasped. "It was Jake!"

As I raced up to him, Kevin quickly stuffed something into his mouth.

But he wasn't quick enough, because I caught a glimpse of it — a piece of hamburger meat. *Raw* hamburger meat.

The blood from the meat oozed down his chin.

Kevin was one of *them*.

One more night until the full moon. I was terrified. But I figured if I stayed in the cabin, I'd be safe.

Then I learned about the overnight trip. We'd hike to a campsite, pitch our tents, and sleep under the sky.

On the night of the full moon!

No way, I thought. I had to get out of it! But how?

On the day before the overnight trip, I told Mum I had a sore throat. "I think it's my tonsils," I croaked.

"Brian," Mum said with a sigh. "You had your tonsils out two years ago."

How could I have been so dumb? Now, even if I really got sick, she'd never believe me.

Next I tried making myself sick by swallowing too much water during swimming. All I did was choke a lot.

Then I tried rubbing what looked like poison ivy leaves on my face and arms. Nothing happened.

Finally, I decided to tell the truth. Well, not the whole truth. I knew my parents would never believe that. So I just told part of it.

"The guys are mean," I said. "I know they're going to do something awful to me. Please don't make me go on the trip. Please?"

Dad crossed his arms. Then he cleared his throat. "Brian," he said, "if I let you stay in the cabin, it would be the worst thing for you. Maybe these guys have been a little rough on you. But if you let them know you're scared, they'll get even rougher."

"Your father's right," Mum told me. "You just have to be patient. Everything will be okay."

"But Mum!"

"That's enough, Brian," Dad said sharply. "I don't want to hear another word. You're going on the overnight camp — and that's that!"

So there I was stuck in the woods with at least four werewolves.

When it started to get dark and the stars came out, I ducked into my tent.

"Hey, Brian, what are you doing?" Kevin yelled. "Don't you want to eat?"

Yeah, right. What was on the menu — raw squirrel?

While the others ate, I stayed in my tent. Pretty soon, the campfire died down. The woods around the lake grew quiet.

Then I spotted a light through my tent. The bright orange light of the rising moon.

The full moon.

I scrunched down in my sleeping bag.

I crossed my fingers and hoped I'd been wrong all along. Maybe nothing would happen.

That's when I heard the first howl.

The hairs on the back of my neck stood up straight. My heart banged away like a hammer. I'd heard that savage howl before.

9

I had to get out of there! I had to make a run for it.

I wiggled out of my sleeping bag. Then I crawled across the tent and pulled the flap back a little. Peeking out, I saw Phil standing in front of his tent in his red T-shirt.

Except he wasn't Phil any more.

Thick dark hair covered his face and arms. White fangs poked out of his mouth, gleaming like daggers. He raised his head to the moon and howled again.

Phil had become a werewolf.

As his howl died down, I lifted the flap a little more. Shadowy figures began to emerge from the other tents. Growling, snarling figures, with thick fur and sharp fangs.

My heart beat double time. I recognized them all. Don, Jake, Kevin and the five other kids in the teen camp. Werewolves! Every one of them!

They huddled around Phil. Formed a pack.

Together they raised their furry heads and howled at the moon.

The sound turned my blood to ice water.

Before I could move, the werewolves turned their wild eyes on me! Their fangs glowed as they began moving towards my tent.

I squeezed my eyes shut. My whole body shook.

Raw squirrel wasn't on the menu. *I* was!

The growls grew louder. My eyes popped open. The werewolves were closing in!

I opened my mouth to scream in terror. But I couldn't make a sound.

I tried to stand, but my legs had turned to jelly. My heartbeat thundered in my ears.

The pack crept closer.

Closer.

Then, Phil's eyes met mine. He put his furry hands under his chin.

And he pulled off his mask.

My mouth fell open in surprise. Phil laughed and laughed. Then Jake, Kevin, Don and the others took their masks off and began laughing, too.

"Welcome to teen camp, Brian!" Phil shouted through bursts of laughter. "We pull this trick on a new kid every summer. But you were the best!"

"Yeah, you really fell for it hard!" Jake hooted. He pulled a little tape recorder out of his pocket and turned it on. First I heard a single howl. After a pause, the horrifying howling I'd heard just minutes before.

"A whole pack of wolves," Jake explained. "It's on a sound effects tape!"

Phil held up the old shoes he'd carved up to make wolf tracks. Don showed me the fake fangs he'd worn during the baseball game.

Kevin held out a plastic bag. "Ketchup and chopped-up spaghetti!" he said. "Looks like raw hamburger, doesn't it?"

Dad had been right. It was all a trick.

I sighed with relief and crawled out of the tent.

The guys all laughed and slapped me on the back. "No hard feelings. Right, Brian?" Kevin asked.

I opened my mouth to say no. But all that came out was a low rumbling sound, from deep in my throat.

"Hey, Brian, the joke's over," Phil said.

Another deep rumble escaped my throat.

I felt strange. Prickly. Itchy all over.

I glanced down and saw the shaggy fur growing on the backs of my hands.

My fingernails grew, stretching into pointed claws.

I rubbed the thick, bristly fur that covered my cheeks and chin.

Snapping my jaws, I let out a sharp growl. Then I raised my face to the full moon — and howled.

Still holding their masks, the other guys stared at me in horror.

I didn't blame them. I used to be scared of werewolves, too!

I let out another long howl. So this is what Mum meant, when she said everything would change soon!

My stomach rumbled. I realized I was really hungry!

I snapped my jaws. My terrified friends all started to run.

But I knew they wouldn't get far. Four legs are faster than two!

I guess Thunder Lake is going to be fun after all! I told myself.

Then I started to run.

P.S. DON'T WRITE BACK

Camp Timber Lake Hills. My new sleepaway camp. My new, really cool, sleepaway camp.

I've been here for eight days now. In Bunk 14. And I'm having a totally awesome time.

The guys in my bunk like to horse around and play tricks on each other. They're the best.

But Sam is crabby. He's the camp director. Sam is huge. Over six feet tall with a stomach that explodes over his belt. His grey, bushy moustache is the only hair that grows on his head. He's totally bald. And he never smiles. Never.

There's lots to do here. But softball is my favourite. The guys in my bunk are the best softball players in the whole camp.

Not to brag or anything, but I happen to be the bunk's star hitter. And I'm only twelve — a year younger than everyone else in the bunk.

Home Run Dave. That's what they call me.

As I said, camp is pretty excellent.

There is one problem, though.

I've been here for over a week, and I haven't received a single letter from home.

That might not sound so strange. But last summer Mum and Dad sent four letters and a tin of biscuits. And that was on the second day.

This year, so far, nothing. Not even a crummy postcard.

So when Sam grumbled, "Mail Call!" this afternoon, I raced out of the bunk. I knew he'd have a letter for me today.

Or a package.

Something.

Sam dug through his mail pouch and pulled out a bunch of letters. "Don Benson! Mark Silver! Patrick Brown!"

The guys jumped up to claim their mail.

By the time Sam finished, Don held up six letters. "Hey, guys. How many did you get?"

Jeremy waved three letters in the air.

Patrick paraded around with the new *Mutant Rat-Man* comic his dad had sent.

I had nothing.

"I can't believe this," I muttered. "Mum promised she would write!"

I know it's no big deal. Really. I mean, there must be lots of kids at camp who don't get mail.

But my parents had *promised*.

Three days later and still no mail.

I asked Sam to check with the post office. He said he would. The post office is run by Miss Mildred. She's been in charge of the town mail forever. And in fifty years, she's never lost a letter. At least that's what she says.

I started imagining all these crazy things. Maybe Mum and Dad sent my letters to the camp I went to last summer. Or maybe there had been an earthquake, and they couldn't leave the house.

Dumb things like that.

Anyway, I finally decided to call home and find out what was going on.

"Sam," I said after mail call that day, "I need to phone home."

Sam shook his head no. "No calls home unless it's an emergency," he barked.

"But it *is* an emergency!" I insisted.

"No calls home."

The next day, after swimming, we all raced back to the bunk to change for our big softball game against Bunk 13.

"Mail Call!" Sam yelled as I did up my trainers. I ran out to the porch in time to see Sam yank out the first letter from his pouch.

"David Stevenson! Today's your lucky day. Miss Mildred found this letter in the bottom of a drawer," Sam said, waving a crumpled envelope in the air. "She can't imagine how it got there. She mumbled something about elves. Anyway, she says she'll keep looking for more."

I practically ripped the letter from his hand. I checked the name on the front just to make sure it was really mine. Then I tore it open.

16

Dear David,
    We're not coming up for Visiting Day.
Your sister misses you. See you in August.
                    Mum and Dad
                    P.S. Don't write back.

Huh? That's it? I turned the paper over, then back again. I gazed around suspiciously. This had to be a joke from one of the guys. But they all had their heads buried in their letters. No one even glanced in my direction.

I sat down and read my letter again.

We're not coming up for Visiting Day.

How could that be? They promised. They *always* came up for Visiting Day. Always.

Your sister misses you.

No way. My older sister Carly danced around the house like a lunatic the day I left for camp. She said it was the happiest day of her life.

And *P.S. Don't write back.* That was the weirdest part of all. Why would Mum write something like that? She said she loved getting letters from me.

A huge lump stuck in my throat. I wanted to cry. But I didn't. Not until the next day.

The next afternoon, another letter came for me.

Excellent! This will explain everything. I started to read.

Dear David,
    We're sending you to live with your Great-uncle John. He's coming to pick you up on the 27th. We think it's for the best.
                    Mum and Dad
                    P.S. Don't write back.

"What?" I choked.

The letter shook in my trembling hands. How can they send me to live with Great-uncle John? I mean, he's eighty-seven years old and lives in an old-age home!

I glanced up and stared into the trees across from my bunk. They started to spin around me. My hands grew numb. Then they turned to ice. My eyes filled with tears.

I leaped up and ran. All the way to the camp office. Up the steps. To the front door. It was locked.

I peered through the window screen. No one inside. But there — hanging on the wall. The phone! I had to get to that phone.

I twisted around to my left. Then to my right. No one in sight. Good. I gently raised the screen and crept over the windowsill into the office. Then I darted for the phone and dialled.

By the third ring, my palms dripped with sweat. Beads of perspiration clung to my forehead.

18

"C'mon! Pick up!" I shifted my weight from one foot to the other. "Come on already!"

Then, finally! On the fourth ring my mother answered!

"Mum!" I cried. "What's going on?"

" — not home right now. Please leave a message. And have a nice — "

Oh, no! I heard voices. Outside. Coming towards the office. No time to leave a message.

Think, Dave! Think! Get out of here quick!

Then I spied it. A window at the back of the office. I threw open the screen and dived out.

I charged back to the bunk. Panting wildly. I leaped up the porch steps. The door flew open.

And there stood Sam. A stone statue. Glaring at me.

"Stevenson! You're in big trouble."

"But, Sam — " I started to explain.

"No, Stevenson. You're late for the scavenger hunt. In the woods. Remember? Now you'll have to catch up with the other guys." He shuffled down the stairs and headed for the trees.

The scavenger hunt. Right. A hike through the woods. Then a campfire supper. Then the hunt. I had forgotten.

I tossed everything out of my drawers, searching for stuff for the scavenger hunt. My sweatshirt. Backpack. Torch.

How could my parents do this to me? I kept repeating over and over to myself as I searched the bunk frantically for my torch.

And then I saw it. Under my bed, *next* to the

19

torch. The envelope. From the letter this afternoon.

I read the address again. David Stevenson, Camp Timber Lane Hills.

That's it! Why hadn't I noticed it before? My camp is Camp Timber *Lake* Hills!

Now it made sense. Camp Timber *Lane* Hills stood on the other side of the lake.

A mix-up. Simple as that. I breathed a small sigh of relief. Those letters weren't for me. They were for some other David Stevenson. At some other camp. And he probably had *my* letters!

I grabbed my torch and stuffed it into my backpack.

I knew what I had to do. While everyone searched for clues on the scavenger hunt, I would escape across the lake and find Camp Timber Lane Hills — and the other David Stevenson.

As soon as the scavenger hunt began, I slipped away in the dark and headed for the dock.

The camp rowboats bobbed gently up and down on the moonlit water. I steadied one and climbed inside.

I leaned over and tugged on the rope that held the anchor. Heavy. Very heavy. I clutched the rope with two hands and heaved.

Uh-oh. Not as heavy as I thought.

The anchor flew out of the water — and crashed on to the boat floor.

The boat pitched from side to side. I crouched

down and grasped the oarlocks tightly. And waited. Waited to be caught.

Silence.

I breathed a low, steadying sigh. Then I locked the oars in place and began to row.

As I cut through the water, the twinkling lights from camp grew smaller and smaller. I turned to glance at the opposite shore. Thick woods. Total blackness. Maybe this wasn't such a good idea.

But I had to get to the other camp. I wanted my mail.

I rowed faster. My arms ached. Tiny splashes around the oars thundered in my ears. My head throbbed.

Then, finally. A dock!

I dropped the anchor and stepped up. The dock's rotted wood splintered and cracked under my trainers.

Where is the path? I wondered, sweeping my torch over thick weeds.

I stumbled through the dark. Through the tall, scratchy grass that scraped against my legs.

Suddenly, the beam from my torch fell upon a big wooden sign. I stood directly in front of it to read the worn letters. CAMP TIMBER LANE HILLS.

I found it!

I gazed beyond the sign. I squinted in the darkness. Yes! Bunks.

But where were all the kids? And why didn't they have any lights in this camp?

21

Weird. Very weird.

I trampled through the grass to the first bunk. A skinny boy, about my age, hunched over the porch railing. He raised his head slowly. His hollowed eyes met mine.

"Uh, excuse me," I stammered. "Is there a David Stevenson in this camp?"

He lifted a bony arm and pointed to the blackened doorway behind him.

"Uh, thanks," I said. But I didn't budge. I wanted to go back. Back to my cheery, normal camp.

Just go in, I told myself. Just get your letters.

I inched past the boy and pushed open the creaky door. My hand trembled as I searched the dark room with my torch. No one here.

I'm leaving, I decided. This place is too creepy. Way too creepy. But as I turned, I caught sight of something. No. Someone. Someone moving in the shadows.

"Who . . . who's there?" I choked out.

"What do you want?" a harsh voice replied.

"I'm, uh, looking for David Stevenson."

"Well, you've found him," the voice snapped back.

I shone my light to the very back of the bunk. And there he stood. A scrawny kid with long brown hair and torn, dirty clothes.

"What do you want?" this David Stevenson demanded with an icy stare.

I couldn't answer. My heart thumped wildly.

"I said, what do you want?" he repeated.

22

I gulped loudly and began. "I have your mail."

His eyes narrowed angrily. "My what?"

I pulled the letters from my pocket and held them out. "Your mail. Letters from home," I explained. "And I'd like mine. If you have them."

"Who are you?" he demanded. He stepped closer to me.

"I'm David Stevenson, too," I replied. "You see, I go to Camp—"

"Leave!" he screamed, shaking his fists violently. "You can't let them see you here!"

Oh, wow! This kid is crazy!

"Listen," I pleaded. "Just give me my letters and I'll go."

"Go! Go! Go!" he shrieked.

I flew out the door and down the steps. The skinny kid had disappeared.

I staggered through the thick grass, darting around tree stumps and boulders.

Then I noticed a familiar smell. The smell of a campfire. I listened. Crackling. Loud snapping.

I crouched down behind a large rock. I spied the flickering light of the campfire. And kids, hundreds of kids, circling it. Arms wrapped around each other. Swaying back and forth. Moaning. Moaning.

What kind of camp is this? I wondered.

I swallowed hard. Something is really wrong here!

I jumped up, ready to bolt. But a long, skinny arm swooped down and grabbed my hand.

23

The kid from the porch! His eyes glowed an evil red as he tugged me towards the fire.

I struggled to break free. But I couldn't escape from the skinny kid's grip.

The swaying campers turned to face us. Moaning.

Their sunken eyes stared blankly into mine. Were they in some kind of weird trance?

They dropped their arms. And parted for us.

My face flushed in the heat of the leaping flames.

And then I knew what would come next. They were going to push me. Into the fire.

"Nooo!" I screamed.

With a hard tug, I broke free. And ran. Faster than I'd ever run before.

I leaped into the boat. I rowed swiftly across that lake. Then I charged up to my bunk.

Sam paced on the porch, back and forth. Back and forth.

"Sam! Sam!" I cried breathlessly.

"Stevenson! Where have you been? The whole camp is out searching for you! And your mother called. She said they had to go away—"

"Sam! Listen!" In one long breath, I told Sam about everything. The camp. The other David Stevenson. The sad, moaning campers. The skinny kid who tried to drag me into the fire.

Sam stared hard at me. "David, what are you talking about? We're the only camp on this lake."

"No! You're wrong, Sam. I saw it. The sign said Camp Timber Lane Hills!"

Sam rubbed his chin thoughtfully. "Well, there once was a camp across the lake," he said. "But it burned to the ground one summer thirty years ago."

"No!" I shrieked. "It's there. I'll show you!"

Sam ushered me up the bunk steps. "We're not going anywhere tonight. We'll straighten all this out in the morning."

"But—"

"In the morning!" Sam repeated sternly. "Now get inside and go to sleep!"

I staggered to my bed in a daze.

"I know what I saw," I mumbled as I climbed into bed.

I grabbed my torch and pulled the covers up over my head. I flicked on the light and flashed it on one of the envelopes that I had just received.

"See. I'm not crazy. It says right here. David Stevenson. Camp Timber Lane Hills."

Then I pointed the light along the top right corner of the envelope. And gasped.

The postmark.

It was dated July 10.

1964.

SOMETHING FISHY

"You mean I have to sit in this horrible, hot flat ALL SUMMER! But, Mum — it's so boring here!"

We always go to the lake. Every single summer. And now she was telling me that we couldn't go.

"It's the money, Eric," Mum said. "It costs a lot to rent a house on the lake, and we don't have it this year."

This had been a terrible year for money. The year of the divorce. The year that everything had gone wrong.

Mum stood in the corner of my bedroom and stared at me. I guess she thought I was going to cry or something. But I didn't cry. I smiled and told her it was okay — even though it wasn't.

After she left, I sprawled on my bed. I closed my eyes and tried to picture the lake. The water was probably bluish-grey today. And clear.

I scrunched my eyes tightly and tried to imagine how it felt. Cold. Nice. I could almost feel the sandy bottom of the lake squish between my toes.

"Eric?" It was my sister, Sarah. Her voice brought me back to my own room.

"Can't you ever knock!" I shouted.

Sarah never knocks. She's nine. Three years younger than me. But she should still knock.

Sarah and I are different in lots of ways. I have brown hair and brown eyes. She has red hair and green eyes. I'm nice, and she isn't. I knock, and she doesn't.

"Well?" I sighed as I rolled off the bed and stomped across the room to my fish tank.

"We're not going to the lake," Sarah announced.

"I know that, Sarah," I groaned.

"But it's boiling here in the city. And we don't have air-conditioning, or anything."

"Don't remind me," I said. "Leave me alone. It's too hot to talk."

She shuffled her feet for a while, but then she left my room. Of course she forgot to close the door behind her.

I gazed into my fish tank and thought about the sweltering city heat. My T-shirt was already sticking to my back. And it was only June. What would it be like by August?

I sprinkled some food into the water and sat down. The fish raced towards it. First the big fish. Then the medium-sized fish.

The little fish almost killed each other fighting over the leftovers.

Well, at least the fish will be able to go swimming this summer, I thought. Lucky fish.

I woke up early the next day. It was brutally hot. It must have been 100 degrees in my room.

I glanced at the clock and groaned. Eight in the morning, and the heat was unbearable. I didn't even bother getting dressed. I just put on my shorts and shuffled out to the kitchen.

Mum was frying bacon and wiping her forehead on her sleeve. "I'll buy some fans today," she promised. She slid a plate of pancakes and bacon under my nose.

I took a few bites. I wasn't very hungry. It was too hot to eat.

I walked back into my room and gazed into the fish tank. The fish seemed fresh and happy. They were flicking through the water like silver and gold flashes of cool lightning.

I wondered what it would be like to be a fish. It must feel fantastic, swimming around like that in the cool water.

I followed the fish for a long time. Back and forth. Back and forth. Until my mother came in.

"Pocket money day, Eric," she announced. "Maybe you can buy something cold this afternoon. Like an ice cream. Or buy another fish. One of those exotic fish that you love so much."

I didn't want to buy a fish. I wanted to BE a fish. In the lake.

I called my friend Benny, but there was no answer. And then I remembered. Benny had gone to Colorado with his parents. My friend Leo was on his way to camp. And Dweezle the Weazel was at his grandmother's for the summer.

Wow. What a boring summer.

I spent my money at the pet shop. I bought a castle for my fish tank. It was pink, with all kinds of doors and windows.

The fish seemed to like it. They swam in and out of it as if it were their new home.

They liked it so much that the next week I bought them a tiny purple rowboat. And the week after that, I bought them a new friend — a plastic diving figure with a long, sharp spear in his hand. They seemed to like that, too.

I gazed at my fish whenever I wasn't at the playground behind school or watching TV or at my computer. I couldn't stop staring at them.

And then, late one night, something seriously strange happened.

My room felt like a furnace. I lay on my bed without moving. My shorts were sticking to the backs of my legs. My socks were clammy and gross.

I turned and glanced at the tank. I stood up. The glow from the fish tank drew me across my shadowy room.

I pulled my desk chair over to the fish tank and gazed at the fish. My gourami streaked through the castle and circled the boat. Again and again.

One of my platys disappeared under the boat.

The bubbles from the filter kept swirling round and round and round. The bubbles faded in and out of focus. Gurgling, gurgling, gurgling.

I raised my left index finger and touched the cool water. I dipped my finger deeper into the tank and twirled it.

My finger seemed to have a mind of its own. It moved in a circle, then drew a perfect figure of eight. It formed another, and then another. Five times clockwise. Two counterclockwise. Three to the side. Again, and again, and again.

In the hall, I heard the clock strike ten times. I drew one more figure of eight through the water with my index finger.

And then, as I sat there with my eyes half closed, the weirdest thing happened.

As the clock struck ten, I suddenly felt wet. And cold.

I blinked several times, trying to understand. I spun around and kicked my feet.

And faced a fish. Eye to beady eye. It was right there, goggling me.

"Whoa!" I cried. "Did I fall in the fish tank?"

I plunged through the water and looked above me. The fish were staring down at me. And they were HUGE! Like whales. Even the smallest goldfish were gigantic.

"How did I get down here?" I gurgled. "What's happened to me? I'm smaller than a goldfish! And I can breathe under water!"

I should have been scared. But this was too exciting!

I couldn't believe it! I dived to the bottom of the tank and did a somersault. Awesome!

I swam around for a long time. I did a dozen surface dives. I plunged down and touched the bottom. I stood on my head. Then I zoomed back up to the top and flicked some water at one of my goldfish.

The goldfish didn't seem happy. His jellylike eyes gazed at me menacingly. And then he began to move. Slowly. Straight towards me.

I raced to the purple rowboat and threw myself into it. The boat lurched and water poured in. But it didn't sink.

The goldfish took his time. Slowly, it began to circle the boat. Round and round and round, watching me menacingly.

Did it plan to attack?

I huddled in the bottom of the little boat all night. I wished the goldfish would stop circling me.

I lost all track of time. After a while, sunlight washed over the fish tank. Morning!

I heard a familiar voice from far away. "Eric? Eric?"

My sister! I was never so glad to hear her voice. "Sarah!" I called. "I'm over here! I'm in the fish tank!"

Peering over the side of the boat, I could see her moving around my room. "Sarah! Over here!" I shouted, cupping my hands around my mouth. "Look in the fish tank! Over here!"

She didn't turn around. She couldn't hear me.

31

I was about the size of an ant. How could I expect her to hear an ant's tiny cry?

Gazing through the glass side of the tank, I saw my sister step closer. "Yes!" I cried aloud. "Yes! She's coming over here!"

She bent down and stared at the fish.

"Here! Over here!" I cried. I jumped up and started waving both arms. I nearly tipped over the boat. "Sarah! Sarah!"

A big gourami floated in front of me, blocking me from view.

When the fish swam away, Sarah was gone.

Now what? I asked myself. I've had my swim. I've had my excitement for one summer. It's time to get out. It's time to get big again.

The enormous goldfish came rolling towards me again. "Look out!" I cried.

Too late. The big fish bumped up hard against the side of the boat. "Hey — !" I cried out as I felt the boat tip. I toppled into the water with a splash.

The fish slid past me. I could feel his scaly skin brush my side. Yuck!

I heard a disgusting sucking sound. I turned and saw the gaping round mouth pulling at the water. Pulling me towards the hungry fish.

I'm going to be fish food! I realized.

I tried to swim faster. But my side started to ache. The sucking sounds grew louder. The fish was pulling me into its mouth.

A desperate idea flashed into my mind. The

32

deep-sea diver! I kicked my feet hard and dived down to the plastic figure.

I grabbed the spear away from the diver — and spun around to face my enemy.

The other fish all scattered to the sides of the tank.

The goldfish attacked, shooting through the water.

I dodged away. Kicked hard. Dived to the bottom of the tank.

I waited, watching it circle. I raised the spear.

I took aim — and sent the spear sailing towards it.

Missed.

That fish was too fast.

I saw its eyes flare with anger. It dived towards me. I pressed my back against the side of the tank. It whipped round and smacked me with its tail.

Stunned, my knees buckled, and I started to drop to the tank floor.

The spear floated down to the bottom. I grabbed it just as the fish attacked again.

The huge yellow body soared towards me. I drew back my arm — and drove the spear into the fish's underbelly.

What am I doing? I asked myself, watching it float on to its side. *I just killed one of my pets!*

But I couldn't worry about it. I mean, it had just tried to *eat* me!

The dead goldfish floated to the top. But I

didn't have time to relax. The other fish were eyeing me now.

I grabbed the spear and held it ready. Was I going to have to fight them all, one by one?

Two neons darted close. They were my smallest fish. But now they were bigger than me! If they decided to attack together, I was doomed!

Then, from far away, I heard voices. The words were muffled by the water. But through the glass, I saw Mum and Sarah.

They were walking about my room. I guessed they wondered where I was.

I knew I couldn't call to them. Especially from the bottom of the tank! But how could I signal them? How could I get their attention?

My heart started to pound when I saw Sarah walk over to the fish tank. She stared down into the water. Then she poked a finger in and flicked the dead fish.

"Mum — there's a dead fish in here!" I heard her call.

I saw Mum step up beside Sarah and stare down at the dead goldfish. Then I saw Mum pick up the white net I keep at the side of the tank.

The net! She's going to use it to lift out the dead fish, I realized.

I took a deep breath and leaped off the tank floor. I started swimming to the top as hard as I could.

I kicked and thrashed through the water. I had to get into that net. It was my only chance to escape.

Up, up, I swam. I reached the surface, gasping, every muscle aching. I grabbed the rim of the net with both hands — and pulled myself up and in.

Yes!

I tried to stand. Tried to wave to my mum. But the net wiggled in the water. It dipped low. I struggled to stay inside.

"Owww!" I cried out as something heavy landed on top of me.

Something heavy. And very smelly.

The dead goldfish.

I tried to shove it off me, but I wasn't strong enough. I couldn't breathe. It was *crushing* me!

And then I felt the water fall away. The net was lifted from the tank. The heavy fish bounced on top of me.

Mum was carrying the net out of the room. I tried to call out. But the dead fish smothered my face.

Where was she taking me?

Oh, no! I knew where! She was taking me to the burial place of all pet goldfish.

The bathroom!

"Please, Mum!" I cried, shoving the dead fish off me. "Please don't flush me! Please don't flush your only son, Mum!"

I climbed on top of the dead fish. But she still couldn't hear me.

"Please don't flush me! I'm in here, too, Mum! It's me! Please don't flush me!"

She tilted the net. I tried to grab the side. Missed.

And went sailing down.

Down, down.

I shut my eyes as I fell. I felt the air whip around me, drying my tiny body.

I waited for the splash.

But my feet hit the floor instead.

Startled, I opened my eyes. I stood face to face with Mum.

She was so stunned, she dropped the net. "Eric! Where did you come from?" she shrieked.

"Oh. Uh . . . I was in my room," I said, trying to sound casual.

But I didn't feel casual. I felt like leaping up and down and screaming. "I'm me again! I'm me!"

How did I get back to my old size? I thought about it a lot that day. I decided that getting dry was the answer. As soon as the air dried me off, I zoomed up to my old size.

And I'm going to stay this size, I promised myself.

I kept the promise for two days. Then the temperature outside soared to 102. I could barely breathe. I needed a swim — desperately.

I stared into the fish tank, remembering how cold and refreshing the water felt. Yes, I knew it was dangerous. I knew what a close call I'd had. I knew that going back in the tank was a crazy idea.

But it was also really exciting. *And* I was sweltering.

This time, I'll be more careful, I told myself. First I got a bag of little stones. I built a wall down the centre of the tank. The fish could swim on one side of the wall. I'd swim on the other.

My own little swimming pool.

When I'm tired of swimming, I'll stand up on the rocks and let the air dry me. And I'll instantly return to my big size.

What could go wrong?

I slid my finger into the fish tank and traced a clockwise figure of eight. I did it five times. Then I changed directions and traced five more figure of eights.

The filter bubbles gurgled ... gurgled ... gurgled. . .

And once again I was tiny, plunging into the water for a refreshing swim.

I had swum for only a minute or two when I heard voices at the top of the tank. Floating slowly, I glanced up. I was surprised to see Mum and Sarah.

"Where's Eric?" I heard Mum ask, her voice muffled by the water. "Where is he? I brought him such a nice surprise."

"Who knows?" I heard Sarah reply. "He keeps disappearing."

Mum leaned closer to the tank. She had a plastic bag in her hand. The bag held two fish. I stared up from the bottom of my private pool.

"Look, Sarah," I heard Mum exclaim. "Eric built a perfect little swimming pool for my present. He piled up rocks and moved the fish to one side. I'll bet he guessed what I was going to buy for him."

"What is it?" I heard Sarah ask. "What did you get him?"

Mum held the bag over the top of the tank. Then she dumped the two new fish into my private swimming pool.

"They are Siamese fighting fish," Mum told Sarah. "The meanest fish on earth! Look at them snap their teeth. Won't Eric be surprised?"

YOU GOTTA BELIEVE ME!

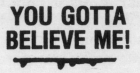

I know you won't believe me. Nobody else does. I told my parents. I told my teachers. I told the police. I told the newspapers. I've even written to the President of the United States. Hah. I might as well have told my pet turtle, Mabel. (Which I did.)

I just saved the world from weird aliens from outer space.

Uh-oh. I can almost hear you thinking, "Weird aliens from outer space? This kid must be nuts!"

But I'm not. Really.

The whole thing started because of the flying saucers. And the flying saucers started because of the no-TV rule. I must be the only kid in the entire *world* whose parents won't have a TV in the house.

"TV rots your brain," my dad says.

"There're plenty of things to do. You don't have to sit in front of a box that tells you how to think," my mum insists.

My parents are old hippies from the sixties. They believe that stuff. So the only TV I get to watch is at Robbie's house, and at Melanie's house. They're my best friends. I try to catch the most popular shows so I don't sound like too much of a geek when everyone talks about them. But I don't watch much.

To make up for no TV, my parents bought me a telescope a few years ago. It was nice of them, I guess. They knew I liked reading science fiction about outer space and stuff.

When you don't have a TV, there's not much to do after homework. So I started watching the sky every night.

And I started seeing flying saucers.

Some were round, with red and green lights. Some were shaped like toilet rolls. Some were big. Some were small. It was truly amazing how crowded it was up there.

Most of them turned out to be weather satellites and stuff from Earth. But others were real. I swear they were. Sure, nobody else saw the flying saucers. But nobody else watched for them.

My mum and dad just laughed. "It must be an aeroplane, Stanley," Dad would tell me. "Or a bird, dear," Mum would add.

"He just wants attention," my older sister, Laura, said. *She* was the one sneaking out early to put on make-up. To get the attention of Herbie, the high school heartthrob.

"Stanley is a geek," offered my little brother, Dan. *He* was the one who made giant balls out of aluminium foil. And *I* was a geek? Hah!

All my teachers thought I was telling stories. And when I called the police, they treated me like a nut.

Then there were my so-called best friends.

"Stan," said Robbie, best friend number one, "you are a total weirdo."

Now, I can tell you that I'm not a weirdo. I'm a perfectly normal twelve-year-old guy. I'm in seventh grade at Piscopo Junior High. I'm one hundred and sixty-two centimetres tall. I have brown hair and blue eyes, and I wear wire-rimmed glasses. I'm good at maths and science. And I play a mean game of basketball.

"He just has a good imagination," said Melanie, best friend number two.

Well, that's probably true. But I don't make things up. Not things that count.

"Look," I told Robbie and Melanie, "I can understand if my family doesn't believe me. I can understand if my teachers don't believe me. I can understand if the cops don't believe me. But you are different. We've been best friends since we were wearing nappies."

Melanie sighed. "Stanley. We *are* your best friends. And we've been your best friends for a long time. That's why we think you should give this outer space thing a rest. There isn't enough room up there for all the flying saucers you've seen!"

And that was that . . . until two days later. Wednesday, July 12. The night that would change my life forever.

It was eleven o'clock, and I couldn't sleep. I felt crummy. It was really hot in my bedroom. Sweat dripped down my neck.

I stared at the green digital numbers on the clock next to my bed. 11:01. 11:02. 11:03.

I couldn't sleep. I got up and trotted downstairs. I poured myself a glass of carrot juice (my parents' favourite drink). Then I stood at the back door. I stared out through the window. It was hazy and dark.

A crack of lightning flashed across the sky. Then came the thunder. *Ka-boom!* It made me jump. Then it started to pour.

At first, I thought I saw another lightning bolt. I squinted and stared hard. Something flashed — but it wasn't lightning.

I ran upstairs to my bedroom. My telescope sat in the window. I pointed it at the flashing light to take a better look. And what I saw made me sweat harder than ever.

A flying saucer!

Round, big and bright. With lots of white lights around it. The lights kept flashing, which is why it looked a little like lightning. It floated above the ground over one of Mr Tribble's cornfields.

I rubbed my eyes. Was I dreaming? I didn't think so.

I pinched myself on the arm just to be sure. It hurt.

The saucer suddenly lifted off and shot away.

Mr Tribble had a bad reputation. He used to chase kids off his land with a pitchfork. He acted mean and strange, and his wife seemed just as weird. Nobody showed up anywhere near his farm if they could help it.

But I couldn't help it. I had to go over there. I had to see what happened in that field.

I pulled on my jeans and a T-shirt. I picked up my trainers.

Carefully, I tiptoed downstairs. I didn't want to wake anybody. I wanted to see what was going on for myself. I opened the front door and sneaked out.

It was still raining, but I hardly noticed. I ran all the way. Finally I reached Mr Tribble's big red barn. I tiptoed over to the end. Then I peered around the corner.

The cornfield was empty. But when I glanced down, I noticed something weird. It looked as if someone had burned a circle in the ground.

I walked slowly over to the burned part. I reached down to touch it. Something had been here.

When I turned around, Mr Tribble stood behind me.

His eyes were glittery and angry. And he was carrying a pitchfork.

"What are you doing in my cornfield?" Mr Tribble demanded.

"Mr Tribble!" I gasped. "Am I glad to see you! A flying saucer landed in your cornfield. Look at those marks—"

"There wasn't anything here," Mr Tribble said sharply.

"But you *must* have seen it!" I cried. "It was here a minute ago. Then it flew away. . ."

"No. Nothing here!" Mr Tribble repeated.

He started walking towards me. His eyes glittered. He bared his teeth. The pitchfork glimmered in the dark.

I ran.

The next morning at breakfast, I told everyone my big news.

"And I think Mr Tribble knows something," I finished. "What do you guys think we should do?"

"Pass the whole-grain toast," Laura said.

"Mrph," Dan said with his mouth full.

"Dan, don't talk with your mouth full," my mum warned.

"Look at this. The factory is closing," my dad groaned. "Another defeat for the workers. It says right here. . ."

And that was that.

My friends were no better.

"Look, Stan," Robbie said. "This has happened before. It's just your imagination."

"Imagination my foot!" I yelled. "Come on over to the field and see for yourself!"

"There is no way I'm going over to Tribble's farm," Melanie shivered. "He is totally creepy."

"All right," I said angrily. "Suit yourself! I'll figure out what to do alone."

And I did. I came up with a brilliant plan. I decided to get my dad's camera and take pictures of the burned circle. Then they'd have to believe me.

Wouldn't they?

The next night, I wore my clothes to bed. I pulled the covers up to my chin so my parents couldn't tell.

I had Dad's camera under my pillow. I was ready. I just had to wait until everyone fell asleep.

I stared at the clock. 11:46. 11:47. I planned to leave at midnight.

I looked out the window. And then I looked again.

The spaceship slid down into Mr Tribble's cornfield.

I grabbed the camera and quietly ran out of the house.

I crept past Mr Tribble's house. I could see the light from his TV through the window. I breathed a sigh of relief. If he kept watching TV, maybe he wouldn't come looking for me.

When I reached the barn, my heart practically stopped beating.

The flying saucer stood there.

It was much bigger than I thought. It was about as big as half a football field!

It was bright and shiny. There were stairs going up into the centre of it. And walking up and down the stairs were THEM.

The aliens! The things from outer space!

They were big, too — the size of Mr Tribble's cows. But they didn't look anything like cows.

They didn't look like anything else I'd ever seen, except in nightmares. Their skin was a mucus-green colour.

They had giant, mushed-in heads with big, glittery eyes. They had tentacles all over their heads where their hair should be. They walked on six legs. Two arms grew out of their backs. And instead of hands, they had giant claws.

A slimy green goo dripped from their bodies.

My mouth dropped open, and I started to shake. I wanted to get out of there . . . fast.

But I couldn't leave. I had to see what they were doing there.

A few aliens held strange-looking silver instruments. Every few minutes, they pointed them at the sky.

And then two aliens slithered right towards me.

Had they seen me?

No.

The aliens started to talk. Their voices sounded gloppy, as if they had bad colds. And to my surprise, they were definitely speaking English!

"We are almost at stage three," slobbered Alien Number One. "This signal will be the final one."

"It is the Earthlings' own fault," slobbered

Alien Number Two. "Sending television waves out into space gave us the idea."

"Once we learned their language," Alien Number One said, "and we understood the importance of television to them, it was just a matter of time."

"It has been ten long years. The invisible messages we have been broadcasting through their TV programmes have made them weak and stupid. Earthlings do not believe in flying saucers. They think we are science *fiction*." Alien Number Two snuffled. Maybe it was laughing.

"This last message will finish them," Alien Number One continued. "They will not be able to resist. They will be helpless before us. They will simply give up."

"When do we broadcast?" Alien Number Two asked.

"In exactly twenty Earth hours," Alien Number One answered. "We start at eight o'clock tomorrow. What the Earthlings call 'prime time'."

I couldn't believe my ears.

All these years, TV really *had* been weakening the human race! Just as my parents said!

Maybe the no-TV rule had been a good idea after all.

The two aliens slithered away. Then I saw a big door open in the top of the spaceship.

All the aliens stopped what they were doing and turned around to watch. I heard a whirring sound. A big silver dish rose out of the ship.

It looked a lot like a TV satellite dish.

That's when I remembered the camera. I had to take some pictures. With my luck, they probably wouldn't come out. But I had to try.

My hands were shaking so hard, I almost couldn't work the buttons.

When I had taken about five pictures, it happened.

I felt a tickle in my nose. It grew and grew. I didn't want to make any noise. But I couldn't help myself.

I sneezed.

Five aliens turned around and stared at the spot where I hid. Before I could move, they darted towards me.

My heart pounded in my chest. I tried to yell. But all that came out was a croak.

I couldn't breathe. I tried to run. But my feet felt as if they were stuck to the ground.

One of the aliens carried a silver bag. The creature took out a kind of tube.

Another alien grabbed me. The first one jammed the tube into my side.

"Ow!" I cried. Then everything went black.

When I woke up, it was dark. I tried to get up, but I couldn't. Someone ... some*thing* ... had strapped me to a table.

I was on the spaceship.

I picked my head up and gazed around. The only light in the room came from a giant TV. It hung in the air about two metres in front of me.

"Just watch the television," a gloppy alien voice said in the darkness.

A rerun of *Space Trekkers* was on. I had heard of the show, but never seen it.

I closed my eyes. I didn't want to watch. But the alien voice said, "Open your eyes, human." Something in its tone told me I'd better listen. So I did.

And I watched.

For three hours.

I expected to feel strange. I expected to get hypnotized or something.

But nothing happened.

I guess you had to watch a lot of alien TV for their waves to work.

Suddenly, the TV went blank.

"How do you feel?" asked the alien voice.

"Fine," I replied in a flat voice. I tried to sound hypnotized.

"Good," said the voice. "Now, go home. You have not been here. When we come, you will be ready."

"I will be ready," I said again in my hypnotized voice.

The next thing I knew, I found myself outside the spaceship. I wanted to run, but I thought it wouldn't be a good idea. I had to pretend to be under the aliens' spell. So I just strolled away, slowly.

Inside the house, I raced upstairs to my parents' bedroom. My legs were weak. My chest burned. I could hardly breathe.

49

"Mum! Dad! There's a flying saucer!" I gasped. "They caught me. And they're sending a TV signal out that will make us all slaves! Tomorrow night at eight! We've got to do something!"

My dad sat up in bed. My mum opened her eyes.

"You had a bad dream, Stanley," Dad told me. "Go back to sleep."

"No, no! It was real!" I yelled. "You've got to believe me. You've got to!"

"Stanley." Mum sat up, too. "It was just a dream. But I'm glad you're beginning to understand why we don't watch television."

"Go to bed, son," my dad said. "We'll talk about it in the morning."

"The entire world is in danger, and you don't believe me!" I wailed.

Then I remembered the pictures. "I have pictures!" I cried. "I took them tonight! They prove it!"

I reached around my neck for the camera.

It was gone.

The next day, Saturday, I called Melanie at eight o'clock in the morning. I think I woke her up. I didn't care. I told her everything.

"Uh, Stanley." Melanie sounded unhappy. "This is really getting too strange. Could you just stop it?"

"I can't stop it," I told her. "I'm telling the truth."

"Yeah, right," she muttered.

When I called Robbie, it was the same story.

"Sure it happened," Robbie said. "And I come from Jupiter!"

I decided to try the police.

"Hey!" Officer Banks cried when I walked up to the station. "It's the flying saucer kid. See another one, kid?"

A couple of the other officers laughed. I just stared at them. They wouldn't believe me, either.

I left the station. I looked around. It was a normal, sunny day. People walked around. No one knew that aliens were about to take over the world. No one seemed to care.

I cared.

And I had an idea.

The aliens had built something to send out their weird waves. Maybe I could build something that would get in the way of them, so they wouldn't reach anyone's TV set.

Maybe I could build a mirror, to reflect the alien waves back at them. I raced over to Robbie's house.

"I need to borrow some money," I told him. "As much as you have."

"How come?" he asked.

"To save the world, of course!" I told him.

Robbie didn't believe me. But he did lend me the money.

So did Melanie. They're pretty good friends. I raced over to the supermarket. I grabbed a cart. And I filled it with every single roll of aluminium foil in the store.

When I got to the checkout, Mr Barnes looked at me and blinked. "What do you want with all that foil, Stanley?" he asked.

"Science experiment for school," I lied.

The total came to $134.59. I didn't have enough money.

"My parents will come in tomorrow and pay you," I told him. *If the aliens don't win*, I added under my breath.

I dragged the foil home to my garage. I started building my giant mirror.

I ran out of foil when the mirror was about twice as big as my dining room table. Then I carried it to Mr Tribble's farm. Luckily, silver foil doesn't weigh a whole lot.

I made sure no one saw me with my mirror. I hid it in the woods behind the barn. Then I crawled closer to see what was going on.

The alien ship sat there. The satellite dish appeared ready.

It looked awfully big. I didn't think my little foil screen would do the trick. But I was running out of time. It was already six-thirty. Then I had another brilliant idea.

I raced home. I crept into my brother Dan's room. And I stole his gigantic foil ball.

I never thought it would come in handy. I guess Dan isn't such a dweeb after all.

The foil from the ball made my screen a lot bigger. I still didn't know if it would work. But I had to try.

I managed to haul the screen up to a high

branch of a big maple tree. From there, I could see the alien satellite dish.

I only hoped the aliens couldn't see me. But they didn't seem to be around. Maybe they were in their ship, getting ready.

I pointed my screen in the right direction. Then I waited.

At exactly eight o'clock, a blue light came streaming from the alien dish.

I held my breath.

The light hit my reflector and bounced right back to the alien ship.

I waited. That's when the blue light went out.

I held my breath.

The alien dish pulled back into the ship. And then the ship took off, straight up into the air. The last I saw of it, it was soaring towards the stars.

I left the silver foil up in the tree. I don't know what happened to it. Mr Tribble probably thought some kids were playing a joke on him.

And then I went home.

What was I supposed to do? Tell somebody? No way.

Maybe the flying saucer will come back. But I doubt it. My guess is, the aliens got a dose of their own medicine. They're probably flying through outer space right now, watching reruns of *I Love Lucy* and slobbering all over each other.

I saved the world from weird aliens from outer space. But no one will believe me.

I finally did tell Robbie and Melanie, a few

days later. But they just asked for their money back.

Then I tried telling my parents, one last time.

"I totally agree," my mum said. "TV could definitely take over the world."

"Pass the tofu," my dad said.

"How do I look, Mum?" my sister Laura asked. "I'm going out with Herbie later."

"You stole my aluminium foil ball!" My brother Dan glared at me. "I just know it."

So that's the end of my story. Unless the aliens come back. And I can get some pictures to prove that the whole thing happened.

I spend a lot of time behind my telescope these days.

Hey. Over there. Did you see those flashing lights?

It's back! Look — the alien ship is back!

You believe me — *don't* you?

SUCKERS!

"Gross!" I shrieked.

Alex Pratt shook the wiggling jellyfish in my face. "What's the matter, Ashley? Scared of a little jellyfish?"

"She's a wimp! All summer people are wimps!" Jimmy Stern exclaimed. He's Alex's best friend.

Alex and Jimmy are fourteen years old. A year older than me. They think they're really cool because they live on Black Island all year round. And anybody who doesn't live here is a wimp.

And that includes my little brother, Jack, and my cousin Greg.

"Drop it on her head! Go on! Do it!" Jimmy urged, pushing his dark, greasy hair out of his eyes.

Alex sniggered. He dangled the jellyfish over my head. Then he lowered it. Slowly.

"Leave her alone!" my cousin Greg yelled. He was hiding behind me. You know, I think they might be right about Greg. He is kind of wimpy.

Alex pushed me aside. Not hard to do. Alex

stands at least fifty centimetres taller than me and is twice as wide!

"I smell sweets," Alex crowed. He moved in closer to Greg. He shoved him back hard. "Hand them over, Greggie."

"No way," Greg replied. "And quit shoving me. Please."

"Yeah," Jack echoed. "Quit shoving him. Or you'll be in big trouble. I take karate, you know."

"The Karate Kid," Jimmy sneered.

"And Sweetie Boy," added Alex. "Get them!"

Alex and Jimmy jumped. They knocked Greg and Jack down into the sand. Then Alex sat on top of Greg.

"Look what I found!" Alex said, pulling out a big bag of sweets from Greg's pocket. He lifted the bag and emptied it into his mouth.

Then the two tough guys jumped up and ran.

"Alex and Jimmy are ruining our whole summer!" I wailed.

We walked along the beach. Greg plucked a piece of driftwood from the shore and hurled it into the ocean.

"I hate those creeps more than anything," he muttered. "I'm going to make them pay."

"Yeah," Jack cried with enthusiasm. "When I earn my black belt, I'll karate them. My teacher says I'm lightning!"

Greg rolled his eyes. "You have about ten belts to go," he reminded Jack. Then he slid his hands into the front pocket of his shorts. His face lit up.

"Hey! They didn't get all my sweets!"

He fished a crumpled bag out of his right pocket. Then he dropped a few of the slimy sweets into his mouth. Greg chomps a few dozen of them a day.

He passed the bag to Jack. "Want one?"

Jack chewed away in silence. Quiet for once.

"How about you, Ash?" He offered the bag to me.

"No way!" I replied. "Jelly worms. Ugh. Totally disgusting."

"You're nuts," Greg replied. "These are awesome. They're the best." He raised the bag to his mouth and gobbled the rest of the worms down.

"Hey, Ash. Look." Greg grinned at me. Little bits of green, purple and red jelly worms stuck to his teeth.

"Yuck! You are disgusting. Totally disgusting. Right, Jack?" I asked. "Right?"

Jack didn't answer. "What's that?" he said, pointing to a big trunk up ahead on the beach. At Bowen's Cove.

The three of us raced through the sand to the trunk. Jack reached it first.

The rusty old chest was as long as a coffin. Draped with barnacles and seaweed. And padlocked.

Jack hopped up and down. "It's a pirate's chest! Full of treasure. Gold and jewels!"

"It's not a pirate's chest," Greg replied. "It probably just fell off a boat and washed ashore. I bet it's full of fishing gear."

I wrinkled my nose. The chest smelled mouldy and sour. "I bet it's full of rotten fish."

Jack danced around the chest. "Let's open it. Hurry!" He slammed the lock with the side of his left hand. It didn't budge.

"I'll open it!" Greg bragged. "Stand back." He lifted his foot. Then smashed it down hard on the lock. Nothing.

I scanned the beach. A few yards away I spotted a sturdy piece of driftwood. I hurried over and carried it back.

Then I shoved the wood into the tiny space between the lock and the lid. With two hands, I slowly pushed down on the wood.

Pop! The lock shot open.

"Way to go!" Jack cried.

Then the three of us started to lift the damp, heavy lid. Inch by inch.

"Whoa!" I cried as it banged wide open.

A big, green, quivering blob sprang out. And flew right at me! It latched on to my leg.

"Help! It's got me!" I shrieked. "Pull it off! Pull it off!"

I shook my leg wildly. But the thing held on. Cold and slimy. Clammy. And as smelly as a hundred dead fish.

It wrapped itself tightly around me. It covered my leg from my ankle to my knee.

"Help!" I yelled to Jack and Greg. But they stood frozen with fear.

I pushed frantically at the slimy blob. My fingers sank into the cold, green gunk. "Ohhh!"

I let out a moan as I felt underneath the skin.

The thing had suckers!

Suckers that twitched and tugged at my skin. And the more I struggled, the tighter they grasped my leg.

THWOCK!

It moved! It dragged itself up my leg by its suckers. Leaving a burning, itchy trail.

"Get it off!" I moaned.

Greg and Jack awoke from their trance. They grabbed for the blob. They yanked at it. But the suckers dug deeper into my leg.

THWOCK. THWOCK.

The blob inched up my thigh. Squeezing harder.

Greg pounded the blob with a stick. "Off, slime-ball!" he yelled. "Off!"

"Greg! Stop!" I cried. "You're smashing my leg."

THWOCK. The blob yanked a moist sucker off my thigh. And wiggled it in the air. Almost as if it were sniffing. Then it nosed the sucker into Greg's T-shirt pocket.

"Whoaaa," Greg cried and jumped back.

The sucker emerged with a jelly worm. Schlop! It sucked the sweet into its slimy body!

"It—it ate a jelly worm!" Greg stammered. "Did you see that?"

"But it doesn't have a mouth," Jack shuddered. "It doesn't even have a head."

Now the blob quivered up my stomach. The suckers jerked at my skin. Would it slurp *me* down, too?

"Stop talking! Do something!" I screamed.

Greg grabbed a bunch of jelly worms from his pocket. He dangled them in front of the blob.

THWOCK. THWOCK. The creature flew off me and heaved itself at the jelly worms. Then it slurped them down.

"Yes! You did it!" I cried.

"But now it's on me!" Greg moaned. "And I'm out of sweets!"

I stared in horror. The blob clung to Greg's arm. Writhing. Pulsating.

Jack gaped at the creature. "I think it's growing!"

Jack was right. The creature strangled Greg's arm and oozed across his chest.

"More sweets!" Greg choked. "In my bedroom. Hurry! It's squeezing me."

Jack and I raced to the front door of our beach cottage. We turned the doorknob.

Locked.

Nobody home.

Jack flung the doormat aside and found the key hidden there for us. He opened the door, and we sprinted up to Greg's bedroom.

"Check his drawers," I ordered. I yanked open Greg's wardrobe door. I pawed through his sweat-shirts and jeans.

Not a single sweet.

"I can't find any in the drawers," Jack cried.

"Check under the bed," I said. "Check *everywhere*."

I dug through the bottom of the wardrobe.

Trainers. Dirty socks. Finally I spied the familiar bags. Dozens of them.

"I've found them!" I cried in triumph.

I snatched up a bag. Empty! Then another. And another. All empty.

"What are we going to do?" Jack wailed.

"We'll go to the shop. Come on — hurry! Let's find our bikes!"

We pedalled furiously to Simpson's General Store.

We dropped our bikes outside the shop and dashed inside. Packets of jelly worms were piled up on the counter.

I snatched about twenty bags. All I could carry. Jack did the same.

"That will be — " Mr Simpson started.

Oh, no! *Money!* I didn't have any money!

"Mr Simpson. Please. I don't have any money. And I need these jelly worms," I explained frantically. "It's a matter of life and death. They're for Greg."

"Greg? He's my best customer. Always buying jelly worms. Okay. Go ahead. I'll charge it to your parents' bill."

"Thanks, Mr Simpson!" I called. We rushed out of the shop.

Jack and I tossed the bags of sweets into my bike basket.

"There's the shortcut to Bowen's Cove," Jack cried. He pointed to a dusty road off Main Street. "Let's take it!"

I hesitated. "Okay," I agreed. "But you'd better be right."

We raced to the road. Then skidded into the turn.

"Oh, no!" Jack cried. "My gear chain slipped. I have to fix it. Go ahead without me. Just stay on this road. Then turn at the cut-off. It's not far."

"Perfect," I mumbled, rolling my eyes. I zoomed down the deserted dirt road. I whizzed by the tall dune grass. So quiet. So still. No one in sight.

And no cut-off for the cove.

I braked to a complete stop. Turned my bike around. "I think I'm lost," I said out loud.

"You're found now."

The dune grass parted. Alex and Jimmy came lumbering out. They gripped my handlebars.

"Roadblock," Jimmy smirked. "No summer people allowed."

Alex peered inside my bike basket. "Yum. Jelly worms. Hey, Jimmy. Ashley wants to share her sweets."

"No!" I shrieked. "I need those."

Alex and Jimmy began tearing into the jelly worm bags. I tried to yank my bike away, but Alex grabbed on to the handlebars again.

Then, Jack came pedalling up. Hair flying. Racing up the path. His tyres throwing huge dirt clouds up in the air.

Alex and Jimmy turned to face him. I quickly moved my bike to the roadside.

"Clear the path, jerks!" Jack cried out.

"Uh-oh. Watch out, Jimmy. The Karate Kid is going to run us over." Jimmy laughed.

Jack kept coming. When he was nearly on top of them, he flung his legs out. And kicked them both into the dirt.

With a cheer, I jumped on my bike. We sped away.

"You'll be sorry!" I heard Alex call after us.

"Yeah. You guys are in big trouble!" Jimmy yelled.

We flew down the road. And there it was — the cut-off to Bowen's Cove! We reached the beach in minutes.

We scooped up the sweets and sprinted down to Greg.

And gasped. The oily blob bulged and quaked. Much bigger. Bigger than Mum's beach umbrella.

And no sign of Greg.

Then I heard a faint cry. "Help me. Help me."

"Greg!" I screamed. "Where are you?"

THWOCK. THWOCK. The slimy blob quivered in the sand. And that's when I saw a trainer. Greg's trainer.

"He's *under* the blob!" I screamed to Jack.

"Can't breathe," Greg moaned.

"Hold on, Greg," I cried. I quickly ripped open a small bag of jelly worms. And placed six sweets down in a thin line.

THWOCK. THWOCK. Schlop!

The slime monster slid forward and slurped the sweets up eagerly.

"More! Open more bags!" I told Jack.

He tore through the bags. And I flung huge handfuls on to the sand.

THWOCK. The blob plucked a slimy sucker off Greg. It quivered excitedly. *Let Greg go*, I thought. *Please let Greg go*.

I threw a mound of jelly worms on the sand.

RRRIP! The monster yanked its suckers off Greg. It rolled forward and slurped down the sweets.

I spun around to Jack. "Lots more sweets. Fast! Try to lead the creature back into the chest."

Greg stumbled as he tried to stand on his wobbly legs. Then he and Jack tore open bags and bags of sweets. I placed a thick trail of sweets in the sand. A river of jelly worms. Leading to the chest.

THWOCK. THWOCK. Schlop. Schlop. The creature followed our trail. Slurping down sweets.

A foot from the chest.

"The chest! Throw some worms into the chest!" I commanded.

Jack and Greg pitched the sweets in.

THWOCK. The blob lurched forward. Inches from the chest.

"Throw the bags right in! There's no time to open them!" I shouted.

The blob wriggled its way up the chest wall. But it had grown too big. Too big to heave itself up.

"We have to push it in!" I cried.

Jack drew back. "*You* push it in!" he shouted. "I'm not touching that blob. What if it grabs me?"

"Not me!" Greg protested. "That thing nearly strangled me."

"But it's our only chance!" I wailed. "We have to boost it back in."

They didn't move.

I threw myself against the creature and shoved. But my hands kept slipping. "It's too slimy," I moaned. "I need your help. Please!"

Jack and Greg stepped forward. Then we all pushed. And pushed. And pushed.

Sweat ran down my forehead. The boys' faces turned a bright red.

Slowly we hoisted the monster into the chest. One oily bulge at a time.

Then we slammed the lid down and jumped on top.

"Hey! Look!" Jack pointed down to the front of the chest. A bag of jelly worms hung out.

"Jelly worms!" Greg cried gleefully. "Awesome! Exactly what I need right now." He leaned over to lift the lid.

"Are you crazy?" I shrieked. "That thing in the chest almost squeezed you to death. Don't lift that lid!"

"Uh-oh," Jack warned.

We glanced up to see Alex and Jimmy angrily charging towards us.

"Jack! Just the guy we're looking for," Alex called. "I think we owe you something."

We scrambled off the chest and headed full speed for the dunes.

I turned back and saw Alex and Jimmy stop in front of the trunk. "Look! Jelly worms!" Alex cried, pointing to the bag poking through the lid. "Excellent!"

"There's plenty more inside!" I called.

Then Jack, Greg and I watched as Alex and Jimmy eagerly pulled up the lid.

DR HORROR'S
HOUSE OF VIDEO

"Help! Help!" Screams echoed through the crowded streets. Something huge and menacing and green rose above the steel-grey city.

A giant monster. A plant monster.

The plant had grasping leaves. Leaves that reached out like hands to grab frightened people below. The people twisted and screamed as the plant lifted them in its leafy grip. Up, up, up to certain death.

I yawned. *Bor*-ing!

I'd seen *The Plant That Squeezed St Louis* three times already. I rewound the videotape. As far as horror movies go, this one just didn't hold up.

And I should know. I'm Ben Adams — I've seen them all. Movies with mummies, movies with werewolves, movies with creatures from other planets. I'm kind of an expert.

In fact, my best friend, Jeff, and I plan to make horror movies when we're older. Right now, we're twelve. Too young to be taken seriously. But we've already made some horror movies with my dad's camcorder.

I usually play the victim. It helps that I have red hair that stands on end and very pale skin. I'm great at acting scared. But what good does that do me now? With Jeff at camp and me on holiday?

That's where I am. On holiday for the summer with my parents. My mum and dad have rented a house near the mountains for the whole month of August. There's nothing to do here. Nowhere to go. And worst of all, no kids my age.

Mum and Dad say, "Go out! Have fun!" But where? I'd rather stay inside, watching horror movies.

And I have. For two whole weeks now, I've been watching videos I brought from home.

"Ben!" my mum called from the other room. "You've been stuck in front of that TV all afternoon." She walked in, then yanked open the blinds.

I blinked in the sudden light. "It's time you got some fresh air. It's not healthy for a growing boy to sit inside all day. I'm going into town for gardening supplies. Why don't you come with me?"

Dad works in the city during the week and is here at weekends. But Mum is a teacher, so she has the summer off. And what does she do? She works in the garden.

"Ben," Mum said in a voice that meant business. "Do you want to come to town?" It wasn't an invitation. It was an order.

68

"But, Mum," I argued, holding the monster video box so she could only see the plant. "I'm watching this educational movie about nature."

Mum rolled her eyes. "That's a horror movie, and I know it. You're wasting your summer, Ben, watching that stuff. Now let's get going."

In town, Mum headed straight for the garden supply store. I gazed up and down the street. I'd never been in this part of town.

Something caught my eye. A video shop! "I'll meet you up the block," I called to Mum.

Hurrying away, I tried to control my excitement. I could get a fresh batch of videos! And best of all, the shop was called Dr Horror's House of Video. It must be all horror movies.

How lucky can a guy get?

I stopped outside the shop. The frayed awning drooped in front. A layer of dust covered the window. I wiped the dirty pane and peered inside.

The inside looked as old and dusty as the outside. Videos were piled everywhere.

Fine with me, I thought. Who knows what I'll find under all that mess?

The door creaked open — and I hadn't even touched it. This just got better and better! Quickly, I slipped inside.

"Can I help you?" someone asked in a low, whispery voice. I whirled around. An elderly man with flowing white hair stood behind me.

He had white bushy eyebrows and a face creased with a thousand tiny lines.

"My name is Dr Horror," he said in that whispery voice. He leaned heavily on a cane, then waved it at all the shelves. "Welcome to my store."

Dr Horror smiled, and I saw that he was missing most of his teeth. "Do you like horror movies?" he asked.

"Are you kidding?" I replied. "I think I've seen every horror movie ever made."

"I bet you haven't seen any of these," Dr Horror said, chuckling. "I make my own in the old garage behind the shop."

I grinned. "Really?" Just wait until I tell Jeff about this, I thought. He'll be totally jealous. Even if he is having a great time at camp, I'll bet he hasn't met anyone like Dr Horror!

"Go on. Look around," Dr Horror told me. "I'm sure you'll find something to frighten you."

This was so cool! I hurried to check out the videos. *Ten Tales from the Mummy Files. Monsters at Midnight. A Boy and His Werewolf.*

"These are terrific!" I said, lifting a vampire video. The vampire on the front had deathly white skin. A drop of ruby-red blood ran down his pale chin.

But it was his expression that really grabbed me. His eyes bored into mine — as if he were gazing into my soul.

Which video should I get? I couldn't decide. They all looked so good!

70

Then I saw a movie playing on one of the video monitors, off in a corner. On screen, a huge monster — half man, half lizard — stepped out from a slimy swamp. He was searching for something to eat.

Squish, *squish*, *squish* went his webbed feet as he spotted a boy in the distance. Lizardman advanced.

I watched, spellbound.

The monster crept closer and closer to the boy. I moved closer, too. The boy's face twisted in fear.

I could feel the boy's fright. I sensed his horror — right in my gut.

Creak! A noise from behind me. I started to turn. But then Lizardman clutched the boy's shoulder. And I felt something grab *my* shoulder.

Something cool and smooth. I looked down. A green hand gripped me. Hard!

"Lizardman!" I screamed.

"Excuse me?" said Mum. She let go of my shoulder and took off a green glove. "I just wanted to show you my new gardening gloves."

She shook her head and stepped in front of the set. "These horror movies make you so jumpy, Ben. I don't think you should be watching them. Let's go home."

I peered around Mum, trying to see the screen.

"Now!" Mum insisted, and she dragged me out of the door.

The next morning I woke up early. I wanted to get to the video shop. I had to see how *Lizardman* ended. But I couldn't say that to Mum. She wouldn't understand.

"I'm going for a bike ride," I told her.

Mum's mouth dropped open in surprise. "You're going *outside*?"

Before she could ask any questions, I wheeled my bike down the driveway and hopped on. Fifteen minutes later, I stood in front of the video store.

A CLOSED sign hung on the door. The store was dark.

I hopped from one foot to the other. When would it open? When would I find out about Lizardman?

I peered through the dusty window, hoping to spot Dr Horror inside.

No such luck. But I did see a flickering light in the corner. A movie played on one of the sets. I squinted at the screen. Lizardman!

"Dr Horror!" I called, knocking. "Are you in there?" I jiggled the doorknob.

The door swung open with a creak. "Dr Horror?" I called in.

No answer.

The only sounds I heard were the voices in the horror movie. And the only light came from the TV.

I'll sneak in, I decided. I'll watch the movie, then sneak back out. No one will even know.

I edged forward, staring at the TV...

An hour later, the movie ended. Lizardman gobbled the boy in a few quick bites. Then he had the other townspeople for dessert.

Cool! Definitely one of the best horror movies I'd seen all summer!

The VCR switched off. The room suddenly fell dark. Time to leave.

I made my way to the door and pulled at the knob. Nothing happened. I tried pushing. The door wouldn't budge.

"Oh, no," I groaned. "I'm locked inside."

Now what? I thought, squinting in the darkness. To my right, I spotted a sliver of light. Another door? A back exit? I crept towards it.

Yes! A door! Behind it, I heard noises. Thumps, and muffled shouts. What was going on?

I leaned against the door, pushing with all my might. The door swung open easily. Startled, I stumbled and fell.

I landed hard on my side. My eyes opened wide. A big webbed foot stood an inch away. Make that two big webbed feet.

"Huh?" I let out a cry and jumped up.

Lizardman in all his green glory towered over me like ... like ... a monster!

A living, breathing monster, flicking his long sharp tongue.His hot breath hit me like a blast from a furnace.

Bright lights beat down on me. Blinding me. I turned to run. Lizardman stretched a long sinewy arm to stop me. He had me in his grip! A grip as strong as an iron band.

I let out a frightened squeal and squinted into the bright light. Was anyone else here?

I heard sounds. Feet pounding.

Hands grasped me. But they didn't pull me from Lizardman. The hands held me in place. Hairy hands. Pale white hands. Hands wrapped with cloth.

Werewolves! Vampires! Mummies!

"Wait a minute!" a familiar voice shouted. I squinted into the light. Dragging his cane, Dr Horror shuffled over. "Hello again," he said.

"H-h-h-i," I stammered.

Dr Horror's eyes gleamed. I twisted hard. But I couldn't break the monsters' hold.

"I see you found the door to the garage," said Dr Horror. He waved his cane around. "What do you think?"

For the first time, I took it all in. The monsters. The lights. The cameras.

I gazed around the huge room. The monsters all looked familiar. The deathly white vampire. The mummy. And, of course, Lizardman. The horror movie monsters!

This garage was their film studio! How could I have forgotten?

I grinned at Lizardman. "Love your work," I said.

Lizardman nodded and released his grip.

"And these costumes!" I went on. "They're the coolest!"

Dr Horror smiled. "Yes, you're a horror fan. Right?"

"The biggest!"

"Good, good, good." Dr Horror rubbed his hands together. "How would you like to be in *Return of Lizardman?*"

"Excuse m-me?" I stammered.

"We're filming the *Lizardman* sequel, and we need a new victim."

Me in a real horror movie? I couldn't believe it!

"Do you have acting experience?" Dr Horror asked.

"Some," I said, thinking of our home movies.

Dr Horror tilted my head and examined my profile. "Well, you seem like a natural. It's a small role. You don't even have lines." He thrust a bunch of papers at me. "Here's the script."

I leafed through the scenes. Lizardman emerging from the swamp . . . destroying a school . . . one boy escaping. "Is that me?" I asked Dr Horror.

"Yes. Any other questions? We're ready to start now."

Now? I wanted to call Jeff at camp. Tell Mum and Dad. Maybe phone a few more friends. I wanted to play this for all it was worth.

"Can I make some phone calls first?" I asked.

Dr Horror checked his watch. "You have time for just one. I suggest you call your parents. We like to have their permission before filming. We can take care of your contract later."

The phone rang ten times before Mum answered. Of course she had been outside gardening.

"I'm not sure," she said when I explained about the movie.

"But, Mum!" I shouted. "This could be my big break. Please, please, please! It's so important to me!" I took a deep breath.

"Just be home in time for dinner," Mum said, finally giving in.

I hung up the phone, then turned back to Dr Horror. "It's all set."

Small alien-creature actors wheeled a swampy backdrop behind me. Everyone bustled around, getting things ready. A four-armed actor plopped a tree right next to me. The vampire and mummy stood behind the cameras. The werewolf set the lights. "There!" he said. A murky glow bathed the room.

Dr Horror motioned for me to stand against the tree. "We'll tie you up," he whispered, strapping me to the trunk. "For your big scene with Lizardman."

"Oh, right," I said, remembering the part in the script. All I had to do was act frightened. Simple enough.

Dr Horror shuffled over to his director's chair. "Now," he said. "You lost your way in the swamp, and fell asleep. When you woke up, you were tied to this tree. You know Lizardman is coming back. But when?"

He turned to the vampire actor running the

camera. "Roll 'em," he said. "Okay . . . action!"

Lizardman crept through the swamp. I tried to look scared. But I was too excited. Too happy.

"Cut!" shouted Dr Horror, shaking his head. "More feeling!"

I tried again. I opened my eyes wide.

Lizardman glided closer. His tail swept from side to side. His eyes darted back and forth. He really seemed hungry. What an actor!

Lizardman flicked out his tongue to catch a fly. Great effect!

And the make-up! As Lizardman slid nearer, I saw just how monsterlike he looked — even up close. Green skin, red bloodshot eyes. Long, slimy tongue.

"Hey, wait," I called out.

"What?" snapped Dr Horror impatiently.

"Don't I need make-up, too?"

Lizardman stood inches away. "I know I'm supposed to be an ordinary boy. But these other actors look terrific!"

I reached up to touch Lizardman's face. "Is this a mask?" Ugh. The skin felt bumpy and cold. It had to be a mask.

"Hey, can I see it?" I tugged at the mask. It didn't budge. "It's stuck," I announced. The other actors crowded around. How nice, I thought. They want to help.

The vampire actor stretched his mouth into a teeth-baring grin. His sharp teeth glinted in the light. Coming closer, he pulled my arms back around the tree. Then he tied them with another rope.

I didn't remember this from the script. "Hey!" I shouted. "What's going on?"

Nobody answered.

Instead, the mummy unwound the wrapping from his face.

I gasped when I saw its decayed flesh hanging from its bony frame. And its eyes — glowing red eyes.

The werewolf shimmered for a moment, growling deep in his throat. He raised his paws, and deadly nails popped out. Two sharp fangs burst from either side of his mouth. His nose quivered with excitement.

This couldn't be trick photography. What was it?

I started to tremble as I answered my own question. These weren't actors from a horror movie! They were *monsters* — real monsters.

"Let me go!" I cried, struggling to get free. The heavy ropes cut into my hands.

I had to escape! I had to! But the ropes held me tight.

I was trapped!

His eyes glowing excitedly, Lizardman breathed in my face. His hot breath hit me full force. A smell like the bottom of a swamp. My stomach turned.

Lizardman's teeth scraped my face. His scaly hand gripped my neck. His tail sliced through the air.

"Dr Horror!" I shrieked. "Save me! Please — *do* something!"

"Whoa! Stop, monsters!" Dr Horror called out. "Stop at once!"

The monsters stepped back. Lizardman froze in place.

Oh, thank goodness! I thought. I'm okay. It was all my imagination.

I let out a relieved sigh. How could I get so carried away?

Dr Horror reached out — to untie me, I thought.

But I was wrong.

He reached up to my head. And he fixed my hair!

"Okay, monsters. Now we're ready for the big eating scene," he said. "Roll 'em!"

THE CAT'S TALE

"Come on down, Marla," my little brother, Scott, called. "We're telling ghost stories!"

"No thanks," I shouted back. Then I covered my ears so I wouldn't hear the next blast of thunder. Thunderstorms weren't so loud when my family lived in the city. Here in the country, the lightning flashed so close — and the thunder boomed so hard — it shook the house.

Last year when I turned twelve, my folks decided it would be safer for my brother and me to grow up in the country. So we moved from New York City up here to River Falls.

Scott loves living in an old house with a big yard. But not me. I hate it. I miss Central Park. I miss taxis. And most of all, I miss my friends.

I listened to the tree branches brush against my window. I suddenly pictured ghosts trying to claw their way through my window and into my room.

I'm not a *chicken* or anything. I'm not even really afraid of the thunder and lightning. I just like it better when there isn't any.

I gasped as the room went black. Now the only light in my room came from the lightning. With every flash, the trees left frightening shadows on my wall.

Downstairs I could hear my parents and Scott still telling ghost stories — in the dark! I wanted no part of *that*.

I couldn't stand the sound of the branches scratching against the glass. I opened the window. Then I felt my way around the room in the darkness. I touched my desk. My chair. My headboard.

"Oh!" I cried out as something big, wet, and hairy flew through the open window. It slammed into my chest — and I fell to the floor.

Long, sharp nails scratched at my arms and neck.

High-pitched screeches rang in my ears.

I stared into two glowing green eyes. Then I started to scream.

Mum and Dad bolted into the room. "Marla, what's the matter?" Dad cried. He held a candle in one hand and Scott's Little League bat in the other.

"A hairy monster!" I shrieked. "It flew into the room! And-and —"

"Is this the monster?" Mum asked sweetly. She held up her candle so I could see. In her arms she carried a small, wet, shaking black cat.

"It's just a cat, honey," Mum said softly. "She must have climbed up the tree and jumped in here to get out of the storm." She examined the cat. "A stray. No tags around her neck."

"Meow!" A loud roar from behind me. I spun around. "Stop it, Scott!" I cried. He laughed. "Meow! Meow!" He thought it was a riot.

I ignored him and reached for the cat. My mother placed her in my arms. "You're nice and safe here," I said to the cat. I turned to my parents. "Can I keep her?"

Mum and Dad glanced at each other. "Marla, a cat is a big responsibility," my dad began.

My face fell. "Please, Dad," I pleaded. "She needs me. She's all alone. And I need *her*. I have no friends around here."

"Well, we'll talk about it in the morning," my mother said. "She can stay tonight, anyway. Come on, Scott, it's bedtime."

I petted the black cat. The storm had stopped. The air was filled with a fresh mist. "I think I'll call you Misty," I said. "And don't worry. You'll be able to stay here — for life! I'll make sure of it."

Misty spent the night curled up at the foot of my bed. And the next morning, she did the weirdest thing. She followed me into the shower!

Misty purred happily as the hot water pounded on her fur.

I'd always heard that cats hate baths and showers. They keep themselves clean by licking themselves.

Not Misty. Misty was special.

When we went down to breakfast, we both

had wet hair. "I see you two have washed up," my father said.

I smiled. Misty also showed her pointy white teeth in a grin.

We all laughed when Misty tried to eat my eggs. "You must be hungry, you poor thing," my mother said.

She gave Misty a saucer of milk and some tuna. "I've spoiled you now," Mum told Misty. "You'll never go for cat food after that." I knew then that Mum would let me keep Misty.

"Kids, I have a great surprise!" Mum said excitedly. "I've joined the swimming club. You two can bike over there today and take a swim. There will be lots of kids your age there."

Scott jumped out of his seat. "All right! A pool! Right here! And we don't have to take a taxi to a stinking old gym. I love it out here!"

I frowned at my brother. He was so easy to please. All it took was a few ghost stories and a swimming pool. I still missed New York.

But since I was stuck here, meeting some other kids didn't seem like such a bad idea. Besides, I love to swim. And the heat wave was starting to get to me. I ran upstairs to put on my swimsuit.

"Hurry up, Marla!" Scott called from the front door. "If you're not here in one minute, I'm going without you."

"See you later, Misty," I said, waving. Misty leaped up on my desk and meowed. She sounded so sad, like a baby who had lost her mother. She cried and cried. I cuddled the cat in my arms and tried to calm her.

"I know how you feel. I don't like being alone in a new house, either," I said, petting her black fur. Then I called downstairs. "Hey, Scott, you go on. I think Misty and I are going to hang out here today."

At dinnertime, Scott told us about the great kids he met at the pool. I felt a little jealous. All I did was read a book while Misty napped.

But when I gazed down at Misty, snuggled in my lap, eating pieces of my frankfurter, I knew I had done the right thing. Misty needed me.

That night I dreamed about my old neighbourhood. My friends and I were rowing a boat in the park. We were having a picnic lunch, and laughing. Then, suddenly, a stranger grabbed me from behind and covered my mouth. I tried to lift my head, but couldn't! I couldn't breathe!

I woke up. I *still* couldn't breathe!

Misty! The cat was sitting on me. Covering my nose and mouth.

I tugged at her with all my strength. But I couldn't budge her.

I started to feel dizzy and weak. The room spun around me.

I struggled to get air into my lungs.

I grabbed at Misty's fur. But the cat pressed even harder against my face.

Beads of sweat dripped from my forehead. My skin turned cold and clammy.

Finally, I curled my hands around Misty's

neck. I ripped her off my face and held her far from my body.

Then I gasped in breath after breath. Holding the cat tightly, I carried her downstairs to the family room. My parents were watching a video. "Mum! Dad!" I cried. "Misty tried to kill me!"

"What?"

"She tried to kill me. She plopped on to my face. She wouldn't get off! She — she tried to suffocate me!"

My mother took Misty from me and petted her back. "Marla, Misty was probably just cold. You know you like to turn the air-conditioning up too high. She was trying to get warm."

Maybe what Mum said made sense. I don't know. But that's when I started getting afraid of that cat.

The next day, when Misty started crying again, I ignored her. I locked the front door on my way out, hopped on my bike, and took off for the swimming club.

The club seemed to be a really fun place. And there were lots of kids my age.

Scott ripped off his shirt and did a belly flop into the deep end. I took my time climbing the ladder to the high diving board.

I was about to dive in. I stared down at the water. And stared again.

For some reason, I suddenly didn't feel like diving. I began to edge back down the board. I didn't want to go in that water.

"Hey, Marla. What's your problem?" Scott called from the pool.

I cupped my hands and started to answer Scott. But I suddenly realized I wasn't the only one on the diving board.

Something brushed up against me and scratched my leg.

"Ow!" I screamed out in pain and surprise.

I lost my balance. I tumbled into the water below.

Cold, blue water poured into my mouth and nose. I thrashed my arms and legs in a panic.

I couldn't swim.

I struggled to reach the surface. But everything went black.

A crowd of people huddled around me. I could hear them congratulating the lifeguard who had jumped in and saved my life.

The lifeguard helped me to a lounge chair. He wrapped my cut leg in a towel. "Stay here," he said. "I'll call your parents and get you some bandages for that cut."

The blood seeped through the white towel. Ow! That was some cut! Who could have scratched me so badly?

Scott raced over to me. I thought he wanted to make sure I was okay.

Instead, he dumped Misty into my lap.

"Mum told you to leave this stupid cat at home," he said. "She followed you all the way up on to the high dive!"

Mum and Dad showed up a few minutes later and drove me home.

"Marla, to celebrate the fact that you're all right, I've made your favourite meal — spaghetti and meatballs!" Mum said.

I felt queasy. I really craved something else. "Uh, Mum?" I asked. "Do you have any of that tuna casserole left? And how about a big glass of milk?"

That shocked my parents. "Are you sure you're okay?" Mum asked. "It's not like you to give up your favourite dinner — especially for leftovers!"

I had a very restless night. I kept hearing whispers. Soft, breathless whispers.

Then the whispers became a creepy chant.

"Nine lives, nine lives. I will have thy body before I've lived my nine. Thy life is mine, and mine is thine."

My eyes darted around the room. No one there. No one — except Misty.

Was I going nuts?

After that, I couldn't sleep at all. I sat straight up in my bed and stared at Misty as she slept.

Had she really spoken?

The next day at the swimming club, I stayed as far as I could from the water. Instead, I joined a volleyball game on the back lawn.

I'm not a great volleyball player. But I managed to spike the ball hard enough to earn my team the winning point.

After the game, Sarah and Melissa, two girls

from my team, asked me to go to the snack bar for ice cream.

"You're a pretty good player," Sarah said. She twirled her ponytail around her finger. "We've got a volleyball team at school. You should join. What grade are you going into?"

"Sixth," I replied shyly.

"Oh, I thought you were older. We're in junior high," Melissa said.

"A mouse!" Sarah cried. She jumped up onto a wooden picnic table.

I saw the little grey creature scurry by. Melissa leaped up next to Sarah.

I didn't join them. I crouched down on the ground and pounced on it.

"Gotcha!" I cried.

I picked up the wriggling mouse by the tail and held it up.

Melissa and Sarah stared at me in horror. "Yuck!" Sarah cried. "That's so disgusting! Get that thing away from me!"

"Eew!" Melissa turned her head away from me. "Marla—*why* did you do that?"

The mouse thrashed about in my hand. I tossed it into the nearby bushes.

Why did I do that? I asked myself.

I hate mice!

Any other day, I'd have been up there on the table with Melissa and Sarah. Instead, I acted really stupid in front of two junior high girls.

I acted like a real jerk. I acted absolutely . . . catlike!

Thy life is mine, and mine is thine.

It was all becoming clear to me. Now I knew why I was afraid of water. Why I had a sudden craving for tuna casserole. Why I found it so easy to pounce on a mouse.

Misty had just about taken over my mind. And, little by little, she was taking over my body.

I'll have thy body before I've lived my nine.

Misty didn't want to share a body with me. She wanted my body all to herself!

I needed a plan. I had to fight back. I had to get rid of Misty before she got rid of me!

I raced home and grabbed Misty by the collar. "We're going for a little ride," I said, trying not to frighten her. Then I placed Misty in the basket in the front of my bike and pedalled off to the local animal shelter in town.

"Don't worry, Miss," the man at the shelter said. "We're sure to find a nice home for a pretty cat like this."

I watched as he tied a name tag around Misty's neck and placed her in a large cage with other cats. Then I cycled home.

For the first time in days, I felt relaxed. Happy.

What a relief! I had done it. I had got rid of Misty and saved my life!

I parked my bike on the side of our garage. I glanced towards the house and gasped. A black cat with deep green eyes stood on the porch.

No! I told myself. It can't be Misty. It just

can't! I locked Misty up in a shelter a mile away. My legs trembled as I walked over to the porch. I lifted the tag on the cat's neck and read it.

Misty! It *was* Misty.

But how did she get home? How?

I feared going to sleep that night. What would Misty do to me? I lay there staring into the darkness.

Then I heard that same, horrifying breathless voice, whispering ever-so-softly in my ear.

"Nine lives, nine lives. I will have thy body before I've lived my nine. Thy life is mine, and mine is thine."

That was enough to keep me awake for a long, long time!

Just before dawn, I shoved Misty into her cat carrier and sneaked out of the house. The carrier had a heavy lock. It could be opened only from the outside with a key.

No way Misty could escape this time! I told myself.

I strapped the carrier to my handlebars and rode through the grey morning to the bus station. The time had come for Misty to take a trip across the country!

We reached the station about half an hour before the bus was scheduled to leave. I watched the morning sun come up over the little town.

Suddenly I felt so thirsty. I set the cat carrier down on the pavement and hurried to the drinks machine.

I had just dropped two quarters into the

machine when I heard the deafening *screeeech*.

The screech of brakes.

A shrill cry.

I spun around in time to see the big red truck squeal to a stop. The driver leaped out of the cab. His face was bright red. "Was that your cat?" he called to me.

I ran over to him, my heart pounding.

"I didn't see her until it was too late," the truck driver told me. "I'm so sorry. Really. Why did you let her walk in the street?"

I opened my mouth to reply, but no words came out.

How had Misty escaped from the carrier? How had she broken the lock and climbed out of the case?

I didn't really care. Misty was dead. Dead and gone.

I wasn't exactly sorry.

That night, I slept soundly, peacefully, for the first time in days. I pulled the covers up high and snuggled my head into my soft pillow. I'm sure I had a smile on my face as I drifted to sleep.

The smile faded when I heard the whispers.

I sat up with a shiver. And listened to the soft chant of the words:

"Eight lives, eight lives left. I will have thy body before I've lived my nine. Thy life is mine, and mine is thine."

SHELL SHOCKER

"Oh, no, you don't!" Tara Bennett yelled to her eight-year-old brother, Tommy. "That's my shell! Mine!"

Tara jumped up from the beach blanket and ran to the shore. She saw the waves wash over Tommy's toes as he rinsed the sand off the shell.

"Give it to me," Tara demanded, wrenching the gleaming white object from her brother's hands. "It's for my shell collection!" she sneered. "The biggest and best shell collection in the world!"

"Not fair, Tara. I saw it first."

"Not fair!" Tara mimicked. She narrowed her blue eyes. "You're a baby."

Tara held the seashell up to the light and admired its smooth curves and pointed spiral. It sparkled like a jewel in the afternoon sun.

"It's the most perfect shell in the world!" she announced. "Everybody is going to be jealous when they see it."

She closed her eyes. And pictured herself back at school. Winning the seventh-grade science fair with her new shell. All the kids in my class will be green with envy, Tara thought happily.

"Can I hold it?" Tommy asked softly.

"No way!" Tara snapped. "You can't even look at it without my permission!"

Clutching the shell tightly, she turned and marched across the beach. Far away from her annoying little brother. Then she flopped down on the sand to examine her newest treasure.

"It's beautiful," she gasped, turning the shell back and forth in her hands. "And it's mine. Not Tommy's. Mine!"

Whenever Tommy found a seashell, he pressed it to his ear. He said he could hear the roar of the ocean inside.

Tommy is such a jerk, Tara thought. She turned the shell over and over in her hand. Everyone knows you can't really hear the ocean inside a shell. Just the same, Tara held the white shell up to her ear.

"Oh, yuck!" Tara cried.

A clump of wet seaweed slid down her cheek.

She wiped the green slime away. Then she placed the shell against her ear again.

And listened.

"Help me!" a tiny voice called from inside.

Tara screamed and dropped the shell.

"Who — who said that?" she stammered, gazing down at the shell. Then she jerked her head up. Expecting to see Tommy laughing at her.

But no one stood there.

Tara sat alone.

She jumped up and backed away from the shell. She stared suspiciously down at it. "Was it you?" she whispered. "Did you talk?"

Don't be silly, Tara, she told herself. Shells can't talk.

Creeping forward, she kicked the shell gently with her toe. It rolled across the sand, then stopped.

"Help me!"

The voice cried louder this time.

Tara screamed again. She began to shiver under the rays of the hot summer sun. She wrapped her arms tightly around herself. Then took a deep, steadying breath.

"Who's in there?" she demanded.

"I'm trapped," the tiny voice wailed. *"Help me!"*

Tara gasped. "I can't believe it!" she cried out. "The shell is talking. To me!"

Tara's head reeled. Beads of sweat dripped from her long blonde hair.

"Of course I'm talking to you. I need your help!" the tiny voice pleaded. *"I'm a prisoner! Please. Pick me up."*

Tara didn't know what to do. She inched closer to the shell. She leaned over and peeked inside. It appeared to be empty.

I have to find out where that voice is coming from, Tara thought. I just have to. Tara carefully lifted the shell from the sand.

"How can I help you?" Tara asked. Her voice trembled.

"Take me to the cave. To help me escape. Please. Trust me," the voice begged.

"Trust you?" Tara asked breathlessly. "I can't even *see* you!"

"Come to the cave. To help me escape. Then you'll understand. Then you'll see me!"

Tara hesitated. A talking shell, she thought. What an opportunity!

She grasped the shell in her hands and smirked. "Why should I help you escape?" she asked. "You're the world's first talking shell! I can make a fortune with you! I'll be rich and famous! People will pay a lot of money to hear a seashell talk!"

Tara's mind raced with all the possibilities. Maybe she would star in her own TV show! Tara and Her Amazing Talking Shell!

"But, Tara, I will talk to you only. When you're alone. So no one will believe you," the voice replied. *"But listen to me! There's something inside the cave that will* really *make you rich and famous."*

"What is it?" Tara demanded, shaking the shell. "Tell me!"

"It's the biggest seashell in the world," the voice told her.

The biggest shell in the world?

Tara pretended not to care. "Oh, really?" she muttered. "The biggest shell in the world? Where is this cave?"

"I'll show you," the voice answered. *"Just walk along the shoreline. To the north end of*

the beach. I'll show you where it is. I promise."

Tara bubbled with excitement. I'll be the most famous shell collector in the world, she thought. I'll be Tara, the Shell Queen!

"Okay," she agreed. "I'll do it! I'll take you to the cave!"

"Yesss!" the voice hissed.

Tara took a small step across the sand. "What about my mum and dad?" she asked. "I should tell them where I'm going."

She gazed across the crowded beach. She spotted her mother and father sprawled out under their neon-pink beach umbrella. Mum turned the pages of a book. Dad slept.

"Don't worry. They won't even notice you're gone," the voice urged. *"Let's go."*

Tara turned towards the north end of the beach. The sun cast an eerie glow over the towering sand dunes. The ocean waves hammered the shore.

"Maybe I'll take Mum with me. There's no lifeguard over there," she muttered.

A loud screech echoed inside the shell.

"Help me!" the voice screamed out. *"Help me — now!"*

"Okay, okay," Tara snapped. "I'll help you. But remember your promise! The biggest shell in the world belongs to me."

Clasping the seashell in her hands, Tara stomped across the beach. The hard, wet sand hurt the bottom of her feet, but she was determined to find the cave . . . and the biggest shell in the world!

Tara walked and walked. "Aren't we there yet?" she whined.

"*Keep going,*" the voice replied.

"But it's getting late!" she moaned.

Tara gazed out over the water. The sun floated on the edge of the sea like a big red beach ball.

"I'm kind of scared," Tara mumbled. "I'm all alone out here."

She turned and searched for her mum and dad and Tommy. She thought she spotted them alongside their pink umbrella on the edge of the beach. Three tiny specks in the sand.

"I want to go back," Tara whimpered. "We've wandered too far."

"*But we're so close,*" the voice said softly. "*We can't turn back now. Look to your right. By the rocks.*"

Tara scanned the beach.

There! The opening of the cave! Practically in front of her!

"Finally," Tara gasped.

She dashed to the cave's dark entrance. And listened. From deep inside the cavern she heard a frightening earsplitting screech!

"What's that?" Tara whispered.

"*It's only the wind,*" the tiny voice explained. "*Let's go in.*"

"But . . . but I'm a little afraid," Tara admitted. "It's so dark in there!"

"*Don't worry,*" the voice replied. "*I can guide*

*you through the cave. Just do exactly as I say.
Walk straight ahead ... and don't touch the
walls."*

Tara took a deep breath and stepped forward.
The darkness swallowed her up. She stumbled
blindly ahead.

The cave floor dipped and pitched. Tara
reached a hand out in front of her. She groped
at the curtain of dark. She staggered on.

A rock. A huge rock stood in her path. Her
foot slammed into it.

"Oh, no!" she screamed as she stumbled. Her
arms flew up from her sides. Up to the walls of
the cave.

Tara shrieked.

The walls. They moved. They squirmed.

With thousands and thousands of black hairy
spiders!

The spiders crawled over Tara's neck.
Through her hair. Up her arms.

Tara leaped away from the wall. She swatted
frantically at the spiders. Their hairy legs
tangled her hair. Pinched her skin.

"I'm getting *out* of here!" she shrieked, frantically batting them off.

"But you can't go now!" the tiny voice in the
shell pleaded. *"You've got to help me! We're so
close now. Don't you want to own the biggest
shell in the world? Don't you want to be rich and
famous?"*

Tara hesitated. Her skin still prickled from
the spiders.

"Wait until you see it," the voice crooned. *"It's the biggest, most beautiful shell you could ever imagine!"*

Tara closed her eyes.

Yes, she thought. The most beautiful shell. MY shell!

"This had better be worth it," she grumbled.

"Oh, it is," the tiny voice replied. *"Just wait. You'll see."*

Tara sighed. She crept deeper into the cave. Slowly. Very slowly.

"Keep walking," the voice in the shell whispered. *"We're almost there. Almost there."*

Tara staggered ahead. Barely breathing. No turning back now, she thought to herself. She had to find this huge shell! She had to have it!

CRUNCH! CRUNCH! CRUNCH!

Something cracked beneath Tara's feet.

"What's that?" she asked nervously. "What am I walking on?"

"Nothing to worry about," the voice in the shell answered. *"Keep walking. But watch your step!"*

Tara took another step and felt something shatter under her toes. "What is it?" she demanded. "It hurts my feet! I want to know!"

Tara spun around and slipped.

"Look out!" cried the voice. *"Don't fall!"*

Too late! Tara tumbled down. Into a huge pile of large white stones. Sharp stones. She cried out as the rough edges cut into her skin.

What are these? She peered closer.

Tara shrieked. And shrieked again.

Her horrified cries echoed through the large cave.

These weren't stones. They were bones. A carpet of bones!

"Nooo!" Tara wailed. She scrambled to her feet. "You can keep your big shell! I'm going home!"

"Wait! Wait! Don't go!" the tiny voice begged. *"There's nothing to fear!"*

Tara stopped. "Nothing to fear?" she yelled. "Look at all the bones in here!"

"They're only fish bones," the voice insisted. *"The tide carries dead fish into the cave."*

Tara gazed at the huge pile of bones on the floor. "Fish bones? They look awfully big to be fish bones."

"They're very big fish," the voice explained. *"But not as big as the biggest shell."*

"Really?" Tara said. Her heart raced with excitement.

She lifted the little shell up to her eyes and shook it hard. "Tell me where it is!" she demanded. "Tell me now, or you'll be a prisoner for the rest of your life. Where is the biggest shell in the world?"

"It's close," the voice told her. *"It's right around the corner. You can almost reach out and touch it. Turn the corner, Tara."*

Tara gasped.

The biggest shell in the world, she thought. It's almost mine!

Tara rounded the corner. She stopped. Listened.

POUND. POUND. POUND.

From the darkest depths of the cave. The beating of a giant monster heart!

"Wh-what's that sound?" Tara gasped.

"It's the pounding of the waves," the voice replied. *"Hurry up now. If you want to see the shell before the tide comes in."*

Tara trembled. She carefully stepped towards the back of the cave. The pounding grew louder. Clutching the shell nervously, Tara inched forward.

A shaft of light filtered down through the cave-top. Tara followed the ray. Down. Down. Down.

And there it sat.

The biggest shell in the world.

Tara's eyes popped open wide with wonder.

The huge shell filled the whole cavern. Its pointed spiral nearly touched the top of the cave. It glistened white and pink. So big. So beautiful.

It stole Tara's breath away.

It was a perfectly formed shell — like the little one in her hand, but a thousand times larger!

"The biggest, most beautiful shell in the whole wide world," Tara whispered in awe.

"See? I told you," the little voice crooned.

Tara rushed forward, hugging the gigantic shell in her arms. It was so big. Her arms didn't even stretch halfway around it! She stroked its smooth pink curves and gazed up at its tall, twisting spiral.

I have found the biggest and best shell of all! Tara thought. "I'll be famous!" she crowed. "I'll be rich! I'll be the greatest shell collector in the whole universe! And everyone will be so jealous!"

"There's something I forgot to tell you," the little voice said. *"This is truly the biggest shell in the world. And inside it lives — the* biggest hermit crab *in the world!"*

With that, the huge shell rose up. Tilted back. And out crawled a monstrous hermit crab!

The biggest, ugliest sea creature Tara had ever seen.

Its bulging red eyes bounced on the ends of two long stems. Its huge green mouth slammed open and shut with a hideous slurp.

Its enormous, cruel claws were the scariest part of all.

They waved frantically in the air. And snapped hard over Tara's head!

Tara shrieked. And tried to run.

Too late.

The monster crab snatched Tara up in its giant claws!

"Help me!" Tara screamed. "Somebody! Help me!"

The tiny voice in the shell burst out laughing. *"Help me! Help me!"* it mocked.

The huge claws of the monster crab pinched Tara's waist. Its pounding heart thundered in her ears. Slimy drool dripped from its hungry jaws.

Tara dropped the small shell to the ground. It rolled across the cave. And stopped.

A tiny hermit crab popped out.

"Look, Mummy, look!" the tiny voice screeched. *"I caught another one!"*

Tara screamed, and the giant claws snapped shut around her.

POISON IVY

Camp Wilbur.

What kind of a name for a camp is *Wilbur?*

I still can't believe my parents sent me here.
"Matt," they said, "you'll love it."

Well, I've got news for them. I don't love it. I
don't even *like* it.

I've never been to sleepaway camp before. I'm
a city kid. Why would I want to sleep away?

I like hanging out with my friends all summer. Rollerblading up and down the pavements.
Hanging out at the playground. Going to the
movies.

I like the city. How am I supposed to get used
to all this fresh air?

Oh, well. I have four weeks to get used to it.
Here I am in a tiny cabin. Not even any screens
on the window.

I've got three bunkmates. Vinny and Mike
aren't bad. They're twelve, like me.

Brad is the problem. He arrived on the first
day with *three* trunks. All filled with perfectly
ironed clothes. Name tags sewn on every item.

Brad has blond hair pulled back in a ponytail down to his collar. He has blue eyes and about a thousand teeth when he smiles. He's real preppy-looking.

As soon as he walked into the cabin, Vinny and I held our noses and cried out, "What's that smell?"

"Yuck!" Mike sniffed several times and made a sour face. He turned to Brad. "What did you step in?"

"It's probably my aftershave," Brad replied calmly. He began carefully unpacking his trunks.

"Huh? Do you shave?" I asked him.

He shook his head. "No. I just like aftershave."

"Smells like sour milk," Vinny whispered. I don't think Brad heard him.

"It keeps my face fresh," Brad said, rubbing his smooth cheeks. "It comes in a spray can. Great stuff. You can borrow some if you like."

I groaned and hurried out the door. How was I going to stand living with a skunk for a whole month?

The cabins are on a low hill that overlooks the baseball field. I jogged down the hill, taking deep breaths, trying to forget that incredible odour.

Some guys from other cabins were starting a softball game. I asked if I could play, too.

The rules at Camp Wilbur are really loose. The place isn't organized at all. The rule is pretty much "Do whatever you want. Just don't get into trouble."

"You can play left field, Matt," a kid named David told me. He waved me to the outfield.

"Anybody got a glove?" I called, trotting over the grass.

"You won't need it. No one here can hit that far!" David joked. At least I *think* he was joking.

"Matt — watch out for that poison ivy," a kid named Jonathan called.

"Huh?" I glanced around. "What poison ivy?"

It wasn't hard to find. I spotted a large patch of the stuff at the edge of the outfield. It was starting to grow over the path that led to the main lodge and the dining hall.

Three leaves. A plant with three leaves. That's how you identify poison ivy. Even a city kid like me knows that.

I gazed at the square patch for a second. Then I stepped away from it and turned to home plate.

Just in time to see the first batter send a high fly ball sailing out to left field. Leaping around the poison ivy patch, I raised my hands and got under it.

"I've got it!" I called.

I didn't have it. The ball sailed over my head.

By the time I chased it down, the batter had run the bases and was sitting in the grass drinking a Coke.

I told you I hate camp.

That night I was awakened by a loud scratching sound. I sat up in my bed and listened.

Scratch. Scratch. Strettttch.

The mosquitos are doing push-ups, I decided. I settled back on my pillow.

But the sound repeated. Scratching. Stretching. A dry rustling from outside.

It wouldn't let me get back to sleep. I climbed out of bed and crossed the cabin to the window. My three bunkmates didn't stir.

I peered out at the purple night. The trees were tall black shadows against the clouded sky. Nothing moved. The leaves didn't rustle.

Something else was making the sound.

Scraaatch. Scraaaatch. Strettttch.

I was wide awake now. I decided to check it out. Silently, I pulled on my high-tops and crept out into the night.

I glanced up and down the hill. Totally dark. Not even any lights on in the counsellors' cabins at the top.

No moon. No stars. No breeze.

I turned and followed the sound down the hill. It grew louder as I approached the baseball field.

Scraaatch. Scraaaatch. Strettttch.

I pictured giant snakes — as long as trains — stretching across the grass.

What could be making that weird sound?

I stepped on to the outfield. The grass was wet from the heavy dew. My trainers slipped and slid.

What am I doing out here? I asked myself. Has all this fresh air warped my brain?

And then the clouds slowly pulled away from

the moon. And as pale white light washed over the ground, I saw the creature.

Its head bobbed on its slender shoulders. Its hands shook on either side of its skinny body.

It rose up. Up.

"Ohhh!" I let out a low moan as I realized I was staring at a plant.

Or rather, a whole bunch of plants — rising up together!

I swallowed hard and started backing up.

The poison ivy patch! It was alive! Alive!

The three leaves formed a head and two hands. They bobbed as the plant stretched on its vine. Stretched over the baseball outfield.

Scraaatch. Scraaaatch. Strettttch.

I couldn't believe it. It was horrifying.

Long tendrils reached out towards me, curling through the darkness. I turned and ran.

I slipped and fell in the dewy grass. But I scrambled to my feet and ran even faster.

I burst into the bunk. The screen door slammed behind me.

"Hey — !" Vinny cried out sleepily.

"Poison ivy!" I screamed. "Run! Run!"

"Huh?" Vinny sat up, rubbing his eyes.

"What's up?" Mike jumped down from his bunk. "Matt — what is it?"

Brad groaned. "Give me a break. It's still night!"

"Run!" I cried. "Poison ivy! It's coming! It's coming up the hill!"

They laughed.

Do you believe it? They laughed at me.

I guess it sounded kind of stupid. And I guess I was exaggerating just a little. It was so dark out there. I probably imagined the whole thing.

Vinny and Mike accused me of having a nightmare. Brad just groaned, rolled over, and went back to sleep.

It took me a while to calm down. But then I fell back to sleep, too. And dreamed about long green snakes.

The next morning, the poison ivy patch had crept over the entire baseball diamond. It covered the outfield and the bases. And it had spread over the path that led to the main lodge.

"Hey — watch out!"

Some guys playfully shoved each other into the poison ivy patch as we made our way to breakfast. Some kids showed off by rolling around in it. They picked up clumps and tossed them at each other. They claimed it couldn't be poison ivy since it grew so fast.

They were wrong.

By that afternoon, about half the kids in camp had horrible red rashes all over. They scratched and moaned and groaned. The camp nurse ran out of lotion by dinnertime!

That afternoon, the poison ivy had spread over the soccer field and the archery ground. And it had climbed halfway up the hill to the cabins.

Luckily, no one in my cabin had touched the

stuff. We sat at dinner at our table in the corner and watched the other kids scratch and complain and carry on.

The sun was sinking down behind the trees when we came out of the dining hall. We saw Larry and Craig, two of the counsellors, carrying weed whackers and weed poison.

"See you later, guys!" Craig called. "We're going to knock out that poison ivy patch if it takes us all night!"

Craig and Larry slapped each other a high five. I watched them make their way into the evening mist, heading towards the poison ivy.

We never saw them again.

Late that night, all four of us in the cabin were awakened by the frightening scratching, stretching sounds. We hurried to the window and peered out.

A thick fog had lowered over the hill. We couldn't see a thing.

I shivered. The scratching sounds were really close. I wondered if I looked as scared as Vinny, Mike and Brad.

We went back to bed. But I don't think any of us could fall asleep.

The next morning, I wearily pulled myself out of bed. I slipped into the T-shirt and shorts I had worn the day before. Still yawning, I crossed the cabin to the door.

Started to push it open.

Pushed harder. Harder.

The door was stuck.

"Hey—what's up?" Vinny called, yawning.

I told him the problem. "I can't get out of the door."

"Then climb out of the window," he suggested.

Good idea. I turned to the window.

"Oh, no!" I shrieked. I *wondered* why it was such a dark morning!

The window was completely covered over. Covered by a thick curtain of POISON IVY!

"It—it's climbed up here!" I stammered, pointing.

My three friends were on their feet now. We were all wide awake. Staring at the heavy curtain of leaves that blocked out all light.

"The poison ivy must have grown over the door, too!" Vinny cried.

As we stared in horror, the ivy started poking into the cracks of the cabin. Long tendrils uncoiled and reached in for us.

"Help! Somebody—help!" Brad shrieked.

"Come on!" I cried. "Let's all try the door!"

Vinny, Mike and I ran to the door and started to shove. We lowered our shoulders to the door and pushed with all our might.

Brad hung back, clinging to a wall, trembling in fright. I turned and saw the ivy tendrils reaching, reaching into the cabin.

We pushed again. A desperate shove.

Yes! The door budged. Just an inch. We could

see the thick poison ivy that had grown over the entire cabin.

"Don't touch it!" Mike cried.

"Brad—come and help us!" I called to him. "Hurry. We've moved it a little. But we need your help."

"Hurry! We've got to get *out* of here!" Vinny urged.

His eyes on the uncoiling tendrils, Brad obediently joined us at the door.

"Everyone push on the count of three!" I cried. "One ... two ..."

Brad stepped to the front and lowered his shoulder to the door.

And to our surprise, the poison ivy appeared to creep back.

We pushed the door open another inch. Then another inch.

"Shove hard!" I cried. "It's retreating or something!"

"We need only a few more inches. Then we can slip through!" Mike shouted.

Brad leaned forward.

The plant backed up.

Brad leaned further.

The plant moved back.

"Why is it doing that?" Brad asked, turning to us.

"I think I know!" I cried excitedly. "It's your aftershave! The plant can't stand your aftershave!"

"That's impossible!" Brad cried. *"Everyone* likes my aftershave!"

"Get the can," I cried. "Let's try to spray the poison ivy!"

Vinny quickly ran to the shelf over Brad's bed. He grabbed the can of aftershave and brought it to the door. Then he raised the can, aimed it at the thick poison ivy — and sprayed.

The can went, *Phhhht.* Nothing came out.

"It's empty!" I shrieked. "We're doomed!"

"No! I have twelve more cans!" Brad cried. "But I don't want to waste them!"

Ignoring Brad's protests, we pulled the twelve cans from his trunk. I ran to the door. I raised the can. I sprayed.

The ivy slid back.

I sprayed again. The ivy slid back some more.

"It works!" I cried. "The horrible smell of the aftershave makes it retreat! Come on, guys — let's get it!"

The three of us edged out the door, spraying the thick plant as we moved.

"Don't use it all up!" Brad called. But his cry was nearly drowned out by the loud *whisssssh* of the spray cans.

Back, back, we pushed the poison ivy. It had covered the whole camp. All the cabins. All of the fields. It had even covered the dining hall.

We had our work cut out for us. But we knew we could do it.

We held our noses and sprayed. Pushing the

poison ivy back. Watching it retreat with every smelly whiff.

Finally, after hours of spraying, we backed the plant into the lake. Its tendrils rose up as if surrendering. And then the whole plant sank beneath the water with a loud *whoooosh*.

"YAAAAAY!" A cheer rang out through the camp as everyone shouted out thanks and congratulations. The counsellors carried my three friends and me around on their shoulders. And we danced and laughed and celebrated.

But not for long.

I was the first to spot the black funnel cloud in the sky.

"A t-tornado!" I stammered.

The black cloud whirled and spun towards us.

But it *can't* be a tornado, I realized. The black cloud was making a buzzing sound. A droning buzz.

Closer. Closer. The buzz grew louder as the dark cloud lowered over the camp.

"Uh-oh!" I heard Brad exclaim over the droning roar.

"Uh-oh?" I demanded. "What do you mean *uh-oh?*"

"I forgot one bad thing about my aftershave," Brad replied.

"One bad thing? What is it?" I asked.

"It attracts mosquitoes," he said.

THE SPIRIT OF
THE HARVEST MOON

Before last weekend, I'd never heard of the Pine Mountain Lodge. Neither had my parents. But then a brochure came in the mail. It advertised the lodge as "Wood Lake's 100-Year-Old Best-Kept Secret."

That's all my parents needed to hear. They have a thing about visiting out-of-the-way places. And the older the better.

"Oh, Jenny," Mum said to me, "doesn't it sound perfect? We'll go in September, over the long holiday weekend."

So here we were. At Pine Mountain Lodge. The only guests here.

"The whole place to ourselves!" Dad exclaimed as he carried in our luggage from the car.

"We'll be like part of the family," Mum said, signing the register. She gave Mr Bass, the owner of the lodge, her cheeriest smile.

Mr Bass grunted. He looked like Frankenstein without the green skin.

His son, Tyler, who is twelve like me, helped Dad carry our fishing poles. I nearly choked when I saw Tyler. He reminded me of a goldfish. He has light orange hair, bulging blue-grey eyes, and skin pulled so thin that you could see his veins right through it.

So far, I had only glimpsed the back of Mrs Bass. She sat like a sack of laundry, in front of the TV.

The only normal-looking one here was Bravo, the Basses' golden retriever. He nuzzled his warm nose in my hand. "You're a good boy. Aren't you?" I said, reaching down to pet him.

"Don't get too many guests here after August," Mr Bass said gruffly. He handed Dad the room key. "Too cold."

Dad grinned. "That's how we like it."

"Absolutely," Mum said. "We love the mountain air."

Mr Bass led us down a long, narrow hallway to our rooms. One dirty lightbulb hanging from the ceiling cast a creepy yellow glow on the walls.

"Well, here it is," Mr Bass said as we approached the end of the hall. He opened the door to two connecting rooms. The first room had knotty pine panelling, a rickety bed piled high with scratchy woollen blankets, and a worn braided rug on the floor.

Across the room, next to a beat-up old chest of drawers, I saw a small, smudged window. On the other side of the dresser stood a green door that led outside.

116

Everything in the room smelled like my dirty gym socks.

I walked through the first room to the second room and peeked inside. It looked exactly the same as the first.

I wandered over to the green door, jerked it open, and poked my head out. It was growing dark out. So I couldn't really see much — just a porch, and, beyond it, trees. Lots and lots of trees.

"Time to close up now," Mr Bass barked. I jumped. I hadn't seen him there.

I ducked out of his way, and he tugged the porch door shut. Then he locked it. Next, he pulled a set of heavy wooden shutters across the front of my window and latched them securely on the top and bottom.

"What are you doing?" I asked.

"Locking up," he said.

"Excuse me, Mr Bass," I replied in my most polite voice. "I like to sleep with the window open."

Mr Bass stared hard at me. "Too cold at night to do that," he said flatly. "Don't want to catch a chill, do you?"

"I guess not," I answered. I glanced into Mum and Dad's room. Their window was shuttered, too.

After Mr Bass left, I unpacked my clothes. He was right. It was freezing up here. I climbed into bed wearing two pairs of socks, sweatpants, and a T-shirt with a sweatshirt over it.

I pulled the blanket up to my chin and studied the room once again. No TV. Just like Mum and Dad to find the one place on the planet without TV!

I spent the next hour or so reading. Then called good night through the connecting door.

"Sleep tight, Jenny," Mum called back. "See you in the morning!"

I guess I was pretty tired because I fell asleep right away. But I kept waking up. I couldn't find a really comfortable position. As I fluffed up my pillow for the tenth time that night, I heard a voice call out my name.

No. Can't be. It's the middle of the night. I plopped my head down on the pillow and closed my eyes.

"Jen-ny."

There! Again! I did hear it! Was it Mum or Dad? It didn't sound like either one of them. Too low and gruff.

I sat up and shivered in the dark. A strong wind rattled the shutters.

"Jen-ny."

"Is that you, Dad?" I quivered. No answer. I knew it wasn't my dad. The voice wasn't coming from his room. It came from outside. From the porch.

"Jen-ny," it cried again. "It's cold out here."

My heart hammered away. What should I do? I crept out of bed to the green door. I leaned my ear against it. "Who's there?" I croaked.

No answer.

I flew back to bed and yanked the covers up to my ears. And waited.

"Jenny! Jenny!" My eyes jerked open. Sunlight peeked through the shutters. I must have fallen asleep.

"Time to get up!" Mum chirped in the doorway. "Did you sleep well?"

"Uh, I was cold," I mumbled. "How did you sleep?"

"Like a rock," Mum sang out happily. "I love this crisp mountain air."

Did I really hear a voice last night? It must have been a dream. Just a weird dream.

After breakfast, Mum and Dad decided to hike up to Devil's Peak.

"Aren't you coming along?" Dad asked as he and Mum buttoned up their identical red-and-black-check jackets. Then they tugged on matching red-and-black caps with furry red earflaps. Boy, did they look stupid.

"Mr Bass says the view up there is spectacular," Mum explained. "Come on, honey. Put your jacket on."

I hate hiking. "Um. Can I hang out with Tyler? And, uh, explore the woods around here?"

"Well, okay," Mum replied. "But don't go too far. We won't be gone long."

Tyler and I played a few games of horseshoes. Then he gave me a tour of the lodge while Bravo tagged along. The tour took two minutes. There was the lodge and then there was the woods. Period.

By now, things were getting pretty boring. Tyler didn't talk much. We sat cross-legged on the porch, staring at each other.

"So, Tyler," I began. "Do you have any friends around here?"

He stared at me with those bulging eyes. "Not really," he answered. "But I don't mind. I like playing alone."

"Oh," I said. I kind of expected him to answer that way. Then I thought about the strange voice from last night.

"Does anybody live near here?" I asked.

"No," he replied. "The next house is a mile away."

"Are you sure there's no one else around here?" I asked. "Because last night I thought I heard someone out here on the porch."

Tyler's body stiffened. "What do you mean?"

I told him about the creepy voice calling my name. "But I'm sure I dreamed the whole thing," I ended.

"Well, you didn't," Tyler said.

"What do you mean?" I gasped.

Tyler moved in close. "There's something I should tell you," he whispered. "I'm only telling you this for your own good. Okay?"

I nodded.

"This lodge is haunted. That voice you heard was the spirit, calling to you."

"The sp-spirit?" I stammered. "What kind of spirit?" I reached out for Bravo and hugged him close to me.

Tyler's eyes narrowed. "A long, long time ago, a tourist hiked up Devil's Peak and never came down."

I gulped loudly.

"They say," Tyler continued, "that his spirit turned into a wandering mist. And the mist takes over a different body every year."

"Really?" I croaked.

"Uh-huh," Tyler said. "A different body every year. At the end of each summer, during the harvest moon, it finds a new body. A warm body. That's why we lock the doors and shutters at night. To keep the spirit from coming inside."

I swallowed hard. I knew we shouldn't have come here. I *knew* it.

"What exactly happens if the spirit comes inside?"

Tyler lowered his voice. "If you let it inside, it will jump out of the body it's in and enter yours. Then *you* will be forced to live on Earth for a year as a wandering mist."

"That's ridiculous," I blurted. "You're making this up. You're just trying to scare me."

"*Jen-ny!*" I nearly jumped out of my skin. I turned to see Mum and Dad waving from the end of the trail. I was never so happy to see my parents. Even in those dumb jackets.

I ran to them, practically knocking them down. "Mum! Dad!"

"Hi, Jen." Dad smiled. His cheeks glowed rosy red from the crisp mountain air. "Did you have fun?"

"Uh, sure," I answered. "I'm glad you're back, though." And I meant it, too.

That night, I didn't look forward to bedtime. But I kept telling myself that Tyler was just trying to scare me. Nothing would happen. Tyler was just a creep. Who had no friends. And I could see why.

After Mr Bass came by to close the shutters, I crawled into bed. I tried really hard to fall asleep. I couldn't.

I was so wide awake, I heard Dad snoring through the door. I hummed along with his snores. And began to drift off. . .

"Jen-ny! It's cold outside."

My eyes popped wide open. I instantly began to shake all over. The voice. It was real. Not a dream.

"Jenny!" it called louder. *"It's cold outside."*

I flew out of bed. "Mum! Dad!" I screamed. I shoved open the door to their room and jumped into bed with them.

Mum bolted straight up. "Jenny! What's wrong?" she cried.

My heart pounded in my chest. "A ghost is after me," I sobbed. Then I told them Tyler's story.

"Oh, honey," Mum said. "Tyler's just playing a mean joke on you. Dad will talk to him in the morning."

"But I heard the voice, Mum. I know I did." I sobbed even harder.

"Calm down, Jen," Dad said softly. "It's only your imagination."

"It is not," I wailed. "I'm not kidding about this. I'm really not."

"We know, dear," Mum replied.

But they didn't know. They had no idea.

The next morning, I shuffled into the dining room. Tired and confused. I sat with my parents, even though I could tell Tyler wanted me to sit with him. But I wasn't going to let that creep near me.

Bravo curled up underneath my chair. As I ate my scrambled eggs, I fed him little scraps of bacon. He took my mind off Tyler.

But I couldn't help stealing a glance at the window. I saw that Tyler hardly ate a thing. In fact, he never seemed to eat much at all. No wonder he was so thin and pale.

Tyler shoved his chair away from his table and headed for ours. Bravo whimpered and nudged my knee. My stomach churned.

Tyler grinned at me. "Want to play some more horseshoes, Jenny?"

My heart began to thud. "No," I said, my eyes glued to my plate. Suddenly I knew. Tyler was pale. Tyler never ate. Tyler's own dog feared him. *Tyler was the spirit!*

"Please, Jenny?" Tyler begged.

"I'm busy," I told him. Then I gave Mum and Dad a look that said don't butt in.

I hung around with Mum and Dad all day. I

even hiked up a nature trail with them. I'd do anything to avoid Tyler.

At dinner that night, I hardly touched my food. On the way back to our rooms, Dad gazed outside. "Look, Jenny! The harvest moon!"

A chill shot through my entire body. Hadn't Tyler said that the spirit finds a new body during the harvest moon?

"What's wrong, honey?" Mum asked. "You look upset."

"I want to go home right now!" I wailed. "If we stay here, the wandering spirit is going to take over my body."

"Jenny," Mum cooed, "you know better than to believe a silly ghost story."

"But there is a ghost!" I cried. "Why won't you believe me?"

Mum just shook her head from side to side. But she walked into my room with me and sat on the bed for a long time.

Then, just before Mr Bass came to lock the shutters, Mum peered out of the window to check the porch. "Jenny! Look!" she said. "Bravo's out there. He'll protect you."

Knowing Bravo sat out there did make me feel a little better. And even though I'm too old to be tucked in, I let Mum tuck me in that night.

"Sleep tight," she said, kissing me good night. "If you need us, Dad and I will be in the lounge playing bridge with the Basses."

"Bridge!" I shouted. "You aren't going to be next door?"

"Jenny," Mum said firmly. "Stop this. You're acting like a baby." Then she left.

I lay very still for a long time. The wind howled through the woods. It blew hard against the porch door. A tree branch scraped against my window. I covered myself with three blankets, but I still shivered underneath them.

I was all alone.

I waited.

Waited for the spirit to call my name.

No voice. Nothing but the sound of the howling wind and the rattling shutters.

BANG! Someone knocked hard on the door. "Jenny. It's cold and windy out here. Let me in. It's me, Tyler!"

I clutched the blankets close to me. He was here. Here to steal my body. "Go away!" I shouted. "You're evil!"

"Please! Let me inside! I lost my key! Jenny, please! Don't leave me out here. It's so cold. Please!"

"No!" I screamed. "Never. Never!" The wind shook the shutters hard now. Tyler kept banging. Tears ran down my face. My whole body trembled. "Go away!" I yelled.

Then I heard Bravo barking. Good boy, Bravo! He must have heard my cries. His paws clattered up the porch steps. He snarled angrily at Tyler.

"Stop it!" Tyler shouted at the dog. "Leave me alone!" I heard Tyler stumble down the stairs.

And then — silence. Bravo had chased Tyler away. The horror had passed.

I was safe.

I let out a long, relieved sigh.

Soft whimpering cut through the quiet. Bravo!

I rushed to the green door, opened it, and Bravo trudged in.

Bravo gazed up at me gratefully. His sad brown eyes stared up to meet mine. "Thanks, Jenny," he said. "It's cold outside."